NINE, NOVENA

WORKS BY OSMAN LINS

FICTION

O Visitante (1955)
Os Gestos (1957)
O Fiel e a Pedra (1961)
Nove, Novena (1966)
[translated as *Nine, Novena* (Los Angeles: Sun & Moon Press, 1995)]
Avalovara (1973)
[translated as *Avalovara* (Austin: University of Texas Press, 1990)]
A Rainha dos Cárceres da Grécia (1976)
[translated as *The Queen of the Prisons of Greece*
(Normal, Illinois: Dalkey Archive Press, 1995)]
Missa do Galo. Variações sobre o Mesmo Tema (1977)
Casos Especiais de Osman Lins (1978)
"Dominigo de Páscoa"
[translated as "Easter Sunday" in *A South American Trilogy*
(Austin-São Paulo: Studia Hispanica, 1981)]

ESSAYS

Marinheiro de Primeira Viagem (1963)
Um Mundo Estagnado (1966)
*Guerra sem Testemunhas. O Escritor, Sua Condição e
a Realidade Social* (1969)
Lima Barreto e o Espaço Romanesco (1974)
Do Ideal e da Glória. Problemas Inculturais Brasileiros (1977)
La Paz Existe? (with Julieta de Godoy Ladeira, 1977)
Evangelho na Taba. Outros Problemas Inculturais Brasileiros (1979)

DRAMA

Lisbela e o Prisioneiro (1964)
Guerra do "Cansa-Cavalo" (1967)
Santa, Automóvel, Soldado (1975)

Osman Lins

NINE, NOVENA

Translated from the Portuguese,
with an Introduction by Adria Frizzi

SUN &
MOON

CLASSICS

104

LOS ANGELES
SUN & MOON PRESS
1995

Sun & Moon Press
A Program of The Contemporary Arts Educational Project, Inc.
a nonprofit corporation
6026 Wilshire Boulevard, Los Angeles, California 90036

This edition first published in paperback in 1995 by Sun & Moon Press
10 9 8 7 6 5 4 3 2 1
FIRST SUN & MOON EDITION
©1995 by Julieta De Godoy Ladeira; ©1966 by Osman Lins
Published originally as *Nove, Novena* (São Paulo: Martins, 1966)
English language translation ©1995 by Adria Frizzi
Published by permission of Julieta De Godoy Ladeira
Biographical material ©1995 by Sun & Moon Press

This book was made possible, in part, through an operational grant from the
Andrew W. Mellon Foundation, and through contributions to
The Contemporary Arts Educational Project, Inc.,
a nonprofit corporation

Cover: Alfredo Volpi, *Casario*
Design: Katie Messborn
Typography: Guy Bennett

LIBRARY OF CONGRESS CATALOGING IN PUBLICATION DATA
Lins, Osman
Nine, Novena
p. cm — Sun & Moon Classics: 104
ISBN: 1-55713-229-1
I. Title. II. Series. III. Translator.
811'.54—dc20

Printed in the United States of America on acid-free paper.

Contents

Introduction

The prominence of Osman Lins's (1924–1978) work is attested to by its repercussions in his native Brazil and abroad, where critical attention, in the form of reviews, articles, theses and dissertations, and several translations (into French, English, German, Spanish and Hungarian) are acquainting a growing number of readers with one of the most innovative writers of this century. Osman Lins's fiction can be divided into two main phases: the first, in a more traditional and realistic vein, includes *O Visitante* (*The Visitor,* 1955), *Os Gestos* (*The Gestures,* 1957) and *O Fiel e a Pedra* (*The Balance's Hand and the Stone,* 1962); while the second, with *Nove, Novena* (*Nine, Novena,* 1966), *Avalovara* (1973) and *A Rainha dos Cárceres da Grécia* (*The Queen of the Prisons of Greece,* 1976), is characterized by formal innovations reflecting the evolution of the author's poetics. In addition to this, Osman Lins's production includes several theater pieces and essays, such as *"Guerra sem Testemunhas"* ("War without Witnesses," 1974), in which he discusses his ideas on art and the task and situation of the writer.

Introduction

Nine, Novena represents a turning point in Osman Lins's work, the relinquishment of a traditional approach to literature in favor of experimentation, and one of the most inventive moments in modern Brazilian literature. It embodies Lins's global, mythic perspective on human existence within nature, while conveying a lyrical intensity in the expansive vision and extreme constructive rigor of its nine component texts. Each has a specific literary configuration; nevertheless, all have in common a number of strategies that are part of a precise and unitary narrative program serving Osman Lins's aspiration to reinsert man into the universe with which he has lost touch. Thus, what gives unity to the nine pieces is not only the recurring themes of entrapment, search for self, art versus life and the mythic aspect of existence; all nine also fragment narration in a manner that privileges the human condition of discourse over the inheritance of stories. They frequently employ ornamentation, lack a central perspective and use graphic signals to indicate narrators. These formal devices constitute Lins's distinctive cultural idiom and give shape to the reading experience.

An approach to the texts of *Nine, Novena* thus requires an understanding of Lins's poetics, which accounts for the way formal innovations serve his complex project: to return us to the mythic through the discourses of culture and the human arts. The paradox inherent in this project and Lins's way of solving it are suggested in his comments on his own work and the situation of the writer. Particularly revealing is Lins's account of his exposure to stained glass cathedral windows and medieval art during his stay in Europe in the early sixties. The art of stained glass windows—direct, synthetic and conscious of its limitations in the face of an overwhelming commitment to spirituality—is for Osman Lins the paradigm of what he aims at in his writing. Another noteworthy feature of medieval art for Lins is its aperspectivism, which, unlike the centralized anthropocentric perspective of the Renaissance, brings about a richer vision, one that is not limited by our "carnal" condition. This lack of central perspective, if applied to the construction of fiction, enhances the reading experience because it does not anchor the contemplation of events to any one narrator or to a definite point in space or time. Furthermore, aperspectivism entails important philosophical consequences of relevance to Osman Lins's concern with a mythical vision of the world and the spiritual force inherent in words, representing the attempt to break away from our human condition and see things from a spiritual point of view.

It is not by accident, then, that the technique of composition employed in *Nine, Novena* has been compared to that of retables, frames often used as altar pieces enclosing a series of painted panels. It is in the aperspectivism of medieval art, in fact, that Osman Lins saw both the experimental techniques of modernism and an overarching spirituality—precisely what the modern sensibility rejects. As in the retable, the law governing *Nine, Novena* is no longer temporality but contiguity—the episodes in the narratives are presented as *tableaux*, and it is the reader

who has to provide the connections between them. This
vision, with its abolition of perspective, distorts the coor-
dinates by which we usually separate reality from fiction.
The result is a non-euclidean, symbolic space and an at-
rophied time, frozen into an eternal present. However,
this stylization of reality, which takes the place of verisi-
militude, is not strictly geometric; it has a strong mythical
basis and thus paradoxically functions to specify the human within the cosmic. This dialectic relationship of geometry and idealism, order and disorder, art and life,
which is one of the central points of Lins's poetics, is
established in the title of the book, which captures the
interplay between the geometrical and the spiritual sphere
at work in the texts.[1]

The structure of the retable in *Nine, Novena* consists of
a fragmentary and non-linear exposition containing a series of micronarratives separated by means of typographic
devices or the shift of emphasis from story to discourse.
In addition to this, the panels of the retable represent
actions already happened or still to come, de-dramatiz-
ing the story by moving away from action and chronological sequence.

While in some of the texts, such as "Pastoral" or "The
Point in the Circle," the configuration of the retable is
mostly limited to a fragmentary textual arrangement, others radicalize it by developing more complex composi-

1 Ana Luiza Andrade, *O Espaço Geométrico e o Espaço Mítico em* Nove, Novena, MA thesis, The University of Texas, August 1978, p. 93.

tions: "Baroque Tale or Tripartite Unity" consists of a textual tripartition articulated by the conjunction "or," which increases the number of panels by adding variants and multiplying the possible outcomes and readings of the story; "The Confused" incorporates in the retable the exploration of the personal pronoun "I"; "Hahn's Pentagon" and "Lost and Found" hinge on the interweaving of several independent stories or retables, and so on.

But the most obvious and complete example of retable is of course "Retable of Saint Joana Carolina," where the model of the retable is adopted explicitly and in its entirety. The story is made up of twelve panels or mysteries corresponding to the twelve signs of the zodiac, and each is told by a rotating first person narrator. All panels, with the exception of the last one, consist of two parts, an introductory, ornamental one and a micronarrative, told as if each narrator were observing or describing one of the paintings. Although the mysteries are presented chronologically, shifts of time backward and forward take place within each segment, involving leaps in time anywhere from two days to twenty or thirty years.

Another characteristic *Nine, Novena* shares with the figurative arts is ornamentation, which appears in the book in the form of rare, regional or technical words, metaphors, "catalogs" and recurring patterns, set apart from the main text by means of content and/or typographic arrangement. The use of ornamentation is not gratuitous. It has two precise functions, the first being to supplement or derive the work's spiritual vision. But ornamentation also emphasizes the world of human discourse by draw-ing attention to its human composition, to the story as created text rather than as a simulacrum of life; it stresses its own artificiality, while claiming its centrality to our as-piration for the spiritual. This paradox, far from calling Lins's project "deconstructively" into question, embodies what is central about human and artistic effort in Osman Lins's view. Ornamentation, in its difference from the very totality of nature it tries to celebrate, not imitate, stands for both a human experience and a spiritual point of view. Osman Lins finds in ornamentation, both as a technique and as an expression of belief, man's effort, through art and creativity, to rediscover, rather than to re-present, the integrative meaning of his mythic relation to the universe. The use of ornaments, then, is particularly important for Lins, who considers contemporary art, with its rejection of ornamentation, fragmentary and therefore negatively charged. It is through this reference to fragmentation that we arrive at the connection between the necessity for or-namentation and Osman Lins's cosmic vision of the world, his idea of ornament as instrumental in the passage from chaos to cosmos. The absence of ornamentation for Lins is a symptom of the fractioning of modern man, who has lost touch with the universe and is no longer capable of conceiving reality in a global way. In discussing the rela-tionship between ornamentation and consciousness Lins refers to the work of Hans Sedlmayr, according to whom the ornament establishes a relationship between man and things, and thus promotes unification. The task of the

writer/artist, then, is that of a unifier, one w
the religious function that in the past bel
priest as agent of the reconciliation of the world.

The instances of ornamentation in *Nine, Novena* are
numerous and function on multiple levels, from objects,
to characters, to discourse itself. Among the most apparent examples are the seventh and ninth mysteries in "Retable of Saint Joana Carolina," in which some of the words
form a typographic pattern, or the ornamental paragraphs
describing the life and habits of insects in "Engagement"
and marine life in "Lost and Found." It is to be noted,
once again, how the ornamental motif becomes a form of
poetic metalanguage inseparable from the theme of the
narratives: in "Engagement," for example, the insects are
both a metaphor for the male protagonist's reification after a life devoted to bureaucracy and an element in the
plotline (they are responsible for the damage to the glass
panes in his office)[2]; in "Retable's" seventh mystery the
plaited pattern formed by the capitalized letters stresses
the motif of weaving symbolic of man's creative act and
of the superior order of the universe ("weaving the
world"); while in the ninth the capitalized words on the
side of the text are reminiscent of miniatures adorning
an ancient manuscript.

The characters of *Nine, Novena,* just like the animals
and plants reproduced on papyrus by the Egyptians in

2 Leyla Perrone-Moisés, Préface, *Retable de Sainte Joane Caroline,* by Osman
Lins, Trans. Maryvonne Lapouge, (Paris: Denöel, 1971), p. 10.

"The Point in the Circle," are not drawn realistically—on the contrary, they are made of words and paper. As a consequence, psychological development and relationships in *Nine, Novena* become elliptic and stylized. What matters most about the characters is not their lifelikeness, but their role as narrative voices, their part in a "higher plan." Thus characterization, like ornamentation, is both a device and a point of view: characters exemplify and dramatize the spiritual referent underlying significant human enterprise; their fidelity is not to the internal coherencies of human motive or psychology.

The plan to which the characters of *Nine, Novena* are subordinated is the aperspectivistic vision obtained through the constant shift in narrative focus. From this point of view, then, the characters, stylized and deliberately limited, unfinished, are merely functional, a fact indicated by their being represented more often than not by a geometric symbol. The polyphony of these disembodied voices constitutes the frame within which the texts are constructed, "a fluctuating world, with successive centers" evoked by the author with the collaboration of the reader, who has to reorder, reconstitute and fill the blanks of the text, thus becoming part of the creative process.

Although the aperspectivistic vision of *Nine, Novena* rules out the possibility of an omniscient narrator in the traditional sense, the presence, beyond the superficial multiplicity of visions, of a "weaving spider" that never relinquishes the control of his narration is apparent. It is this narrator who weaves his web with the voices he himself emits: a ventriloquist voice breaking into often fast-paced alternations or duets, as in "Retable's" ninth mystery and the first segment of "Hahn's Pentagon"; choruses reminiscent of the Greek tragedy, as in "Lost and Found" and "Retable"; or a figure who bifurcates the "I" or fuses two different ones ("Baroque Tale" and "The Confused" respectively).

Osman Lins's desire to move away from the laws governing the traditional structures of prose fiction is not limited to characters only, but involves an overall effort to shift the emphasis from "story" to "discourse." His attitude about fiction writing can be thus summarized: on the one hand, he acknowledges that the story is the raw material and supporting frame of the novel; on the other, he deliberately chooses not to make it the focus of his writing, whose declared purpose, as we have seen, is to reinsert man in the universe with which he has lost touch. This shift of emphasis—from the sequence of events to the conditions of human articulation within the context of spirit—is effected by the fragmentation of the story, its interruption by discursive detours, stylization and abstraction, which delay and deny the sequence upon which the story depends.

The relevance of discourse over story, apparent on all levels of the text, also surfaces in Lins's style, exasperatingly cerebral and lyrical at the same time. The sentences are long, stretched to their (and the reader's) limit, broken up by countless parenthetical clauses and heavily punctuated. Osman Lins's systematic disruption of continuity thus forces the reader to restructure her/his expectations by deferring the delivery of the information—the story—and drawing attention to discourse and its acrobatics. This style, full of afterthoughts and clarifications, detailed descriptions, ornamental passages and motifs and catalogs, literally smothers the story, constantly denying its primacy in the text. The effect of atemporality or "presentification" is mainly the result of the predominance of the present tense in the texts, often regardless of the position in time of the events or their order with respect to one another. Even when other tenses are used, the abrupt shift from one to another and the inconsistency in their use shatters the fictional illusion by disrupting the chronological succession of events and evoking "a huge present swallowing past and future."

In addition, Osman Lins makes use of a series of graphic signals which function as a reading aid. Some of them—squares, circles, triangles, parallel lines, etc.—are taken from the realm of geometry, others are the author's invention. Many also have traditional symbolic connotations, such as the square, representing the four elements and thus matter, earth and balance; or the triangle, which stands for the spirit (Andrade, 47). The signals further segment the story and syntax, alert the reader to changes of voice and scenario in the text, render the narrator even more abstract by depriving him/her of a name and, at the same time, impart a musical order to the reading by marking the entrance of each voice or the simultaneous emission of voices by the fusion of symbols, as in the beginning of "Hahn's Pentagon."

The apparent paradox of Osman Lins's poetics, hinging on fragmentation on one hand and elaborate patterns and schemes on the other, is clarified by the philosophic vision that informs such poetics. Thus the fragmentation of discourse reflects the chaos of the world, and the geometric organization the cosmic order which can be achieved by art. This aspiration to unity and the basic idea of passage from flesh to logos, from chaos to order, is expressed on every level of the texts by means of self-reflective metaphors developed within the fiction itself. An example is "Point in the Circle," where the encounter of the man and the woman corresponds to a "geometrical metaphor" in which the fixity of the point, representing the order of the creator, and the dynamic of the circle (the chaos of the world) are brought together by the contemplation of eternity through the artist's glass eye, symbol of the incorruptible and "artificial" nature of the written word.[3]

It is in the context of this integrative project, then, that we are to see the mythic overtones and the archetypal dimension of many of the characters, which go beyond the here and now of the story. Characters such as Joana

3 Ana Luiza Andrade, *As Narrativas de Osman Lins: Crítica e Criação*, Diss. The University of Texas at Austin, 1982, p. 286. See also, by the same author, *Osman Lins: Crítica e Criação*, (São Paulo: Hucitec, 1987).

Carolina, who as a child plays with scorpions without getting stung; her husband and children, who catch and train birds; Baltazar, who is made of vines and shares his solitude with his mare Canária; and z.i., who is made of insects, epitomize the mythic integration of man and nature. This relationship of mutual solidarity between man and nature is made stronger by the consistent presence of the world—the cosmos—as such in the texts. Examples of this are the sea and the geological eras in "Lost and Found," associated with the cycle of death and renovation; the pattern of the zodiacal signs and the circular time of constellations in "Retable"; the insects in "Engagement"; the hurricane in "Point"; and so on. This aspiration to the unity of man and world reaches one of its highest points in "Retable's" final mystery, where Osman Lins achieves the balance of old and new, geometry and life, myth and reality in an intensely lyrical, yet carefully planned verbal tour de force which literally brings together men and nature by means of words that are both proper names and nouns designating animals and plants.

A note on the translation: the choices I made were mostly determined by my desire to translate not only Osman Lins's meaning but also his style. Hence the elliptical, heavily punctuated style of the translation, full of inversions and tense shifts, which attempts to reflect the tone and rhythm of Lins's original texts.

I would like to thank João Alexandre Barbosa and Julieta de Godoy Ladeira for their interest in and support of this project, as well as David Jackson, Fred Ellison and Wayne Lesser for their comments and suggestions. I am especially grateful to R.E. Young for his patience and for reading and suggesting improvements to the manuscript throughout its evolution.

—ADRIA FRIZZI

The water, the wind, the light,
on one side the river, up above the clouds,
rooted in nature the building
growing out of its simple forces.

    —João Cabral de Melo Neto,
      O Engenheiro

A clear and synthetic geometrical conception
always provides a good plan.

    —Matila C. Ghyka,
      Esthétique des Proportions dans la Nature
      et dans les Arts

The Transparent Bird

Undefined, an eight-year-old face. Fine, light hair falling on his forehead. Pensive, leaning out of the kitchen window, he watches the black and white cat sitting on the wall. Perhaps there is a hidden sadness in his eyes and, around his lips, lines of premature resignation. The two, cat and boy, look at each other. Reverberations of suppressed anger and arrogance flicker across his face. Arrogance without firmness, something elastic and insecure at the same time: a loose spring.

You are looking down on me because you are on the wall. But I am going to be a man, I am going to live a hundred years. I am going to grow up. And when I am taller than doors and roofs, where will you be? Huh? Sitting where? I look at you and I can already see a pile of bones gleaming in the garbage dump. You walk softly, you are a walking silence. When *I* grow up, my heels will strike the ground like thunder. I will shout out loud, in a voice sonorous as a bell. And you, proud one?

The cat and its profile have vanished, no point in looking for the little boy's features in this man's exhausted face, framed by the train window. His dark hair is starting to gray, his black worsted suit (mourning for his father) is too loose, too comfortable, his white socks are falling around his ankles, his shoes dusty. In the baggage net above him is his dingy black briefcase filled with papers and money, his umbrella with the metal handle, and the gray hat, the round trip ticket stuck in its band. How many years has it been since I tore up those letters, one by one, on this same train? And how long have I been seeing the same landscape—two, three times a month, at dawn and in the evening? It has changed very little, unlike me. And my change, was it for better or worse? How would that young man act during the scene that will take place tonight: my relatives and their vain plea for mercy? This sugar plantation, like the others I see along the road, looks eternal, with its sad chimney, its old tile roofs and dark shed. It seems as if the same men, forever little boys, were watching the train go by. As if the cows, in the pasture, were the same. Only the trees change, because of summer and the rainy season, they regain their beauty every year. Man's youth, fortunately, is not like the leaves of these trees. If it were, if I were young again, I would certainly make the same mistakes, perhaps others, even bigger.

The light in the living room is yellow and pasty. Even if we used stronger bulbs it would be the same, the town's generator is second-rate, old, short of breath, and works as slowly as the town itself. Dinner was over an hour ago, the three children's places are empty, they are asleep. Sit-

ting at one end of the long table, from which the maid
has yet to clear the coffee cups, the empty butter dish,
plates and silverware (she will only after everybody gets
up, as she has been instructed) the man, without his tie,
his shirt sleeves rolled up, impassively listens to the arguments of an old woman in black. A large old-fashioned
silver brooch with the portrait of her late husband is
pinned on the collar of her dress. The two girls look at
her with hope, but it is obvious that the young man is
ashamed, that he would sacrifice many things not to suffer
this humiliation. From the other end of the table, the man
feels his wife's exacting eyes fixed on him, as if screaming: "Don't listen to her, do like the other times. Compassion costs money."

You are wasting your time, Eudóxia. You are wasting
your time looking at me like this, as if I were a roulette
ball about to stop on a number you did not bet on. Don't
you know me yet? Haven't you gotten used to the pained
expression with which I listen to lamentations like this?
Must I stamp on my face the decision I keep inside, a
decision made before she even thought of coming, bringing along, to move me to compassion, her three children
and this brooch on which we see the profile of my mother's
brother? I will not give in, even though, for today, I will
give them some hope. But I will not let them off, all the
papers are legal and in my name, in a few days the house
where they live will be mine, we will be richer, we have
children, three, we have to leave them something. This
woman, the young man, the two girls, will stay on for a

few months, for free, in the house they used to own and that will not belong to them any more. No more. This way, I will do them a favor, which will work to our advantage for a few months, while people still remember the fact and could, for that reason, accuse us. These four, then, will think that I am heartless, but not terribly so, and even a little naive. Then I will throw them out.

Even though he is convinced of the contrary, he is still a child. Naked from the waist up, locked in his room, on the same bed he left two years and ten months ago— promising to himself he would not come back until his dreams came true, until he had had the opportunity to throw his success in the face of all those miserable relatives who never believed in him—that bed, which will have to be changed because his bones have grown. He is kneeling, his back arched, his face pressed against the sheet, between his cold hands. A bent steel bar, tense as if striving to recover its rectilinear form, a sob shakes his body.

They have won. It is hard to accept, but true, I have lost. I did not have the courage. Once again these odious orders, once again this lethargic town, these streets that only an earthquake could change, once again this life I loathe, wilted and hollow, this condemnation. I should get up, change my clothes, hop on the first truck passing on the road, clench my teeth and go somewhere. Like that day. I should take the leap again. With more determination, this time. But I will not go. Why couldn't I endure hunger, why didn't I let myself die? They would sigh with relief, smugly saying to themselves that you must not dare because the price is death, but deep inside they would have to accept the truth: "He acted like a man. He didn't succeed in the jobs he took, in his dubious ventures, he didn't have any help, he died penniless, but he accepted the consequences of his decision. In this respect he won." They would not have the right to smile, to look at me with irony, pity, complaisance and a kind of satiety, as if they all had ravenously devoured my capitulation. I am going to accept the destiny they have assigned me. But I will show them who I am. One day they will say that it would have been better if I had gone away. They are going to disappear. I will be the king, the master of them all.

Two faces, one derisive and solemn, seen in profile on the raised pillow, a handkerchief tied under its jaw, the other frontal, sarcastically looking at the dead man, both immobile. The profile—it was not like this when he was alive: clearly defined—has a youthful air about it, despite the moustache the color of dirty silver; the observer, on the contrary, looks old, so that the two almost seem overlaying studies of the same face—one at rest, the other alert.

Yes, father. I have wanted to see you like this for years, broken, powerless, that authoritarian voice of yours silenced, ever since the day when, forsaken, I felt your inclemency and decided to come back. There always was a dead man within you: this. He ran your life, established the laws I had to obey. I was the son, I had the obligation to receive—inherit—not only the things you prized and conquered, but also your attachment to those assets which, by your standards, stood for the grandiose and eternal: the warehouse, the rent houses, the reputation of being a just man, a life without love or adventure, the town, the habit of running other peoples' lives. Well, I got the inheritance. I gave up forever my right to live my own life. I married the woman you decided was right for me, I am saturated with everything I loathe, I have become corrupted, I like to be respected, to own riches that will grow even larger, I carry you inside me, I will never leave this town. I am the continuator, the vassal, the son. The father.

The young woman, her left elbow resting on her right hand, her left hand free to gesture—the same old posture—smiles and nods toward the sea.

—There it is. After all these years, I'm going to cross it.

—I've seen your name in the papers. I read that you'd gotten a scholarship to go to Spain. I was glad, I said to myself: "Look at that, who would have guessed that she'd become a famous artist." The paper published photographs of some of your paintings—fruit, birds flying. One was transparent, you could see the bird and its heart. It looked like a bird of prey.

—And it had the eyes of a man.

—Right. It was scary. Does that bird exist?

—No.

Boards creaking, the gentle rocking of a ship, phrases in a strange tongue, windward, yelled out by the sailors.

—You didn't draw, back then.

—I wrote poetry. I never showed it to you.

—Sometimes, when I have the time, I come to the port and watch the steamships. I never go aboard, though. And you're going to travel. I'd like to see more of your drawings.

—When I put on an exhibit, I'll send you an invitation.

—My father died a long time ago, did you hear about it? I took over his business, I live in the house that used to be his. The address...

—I know it. You'll get the invitation.

—I'd like to ask you a favor. Send me a postcard from Spain. A card with the Gypsies of Granada.

—How shall I sign it?

—What do you take me for? Sign as you wish. Your name or any other. Or none.

—I'll put a man's name.

—Since it comes from Granada I'll know who sent it. Just think! Who could have guessed? Do you know that once, opening a drawer, I, too, found some verses of mine? Incredible. I had forgotten all about them. How we change!

—I don't think I've changed much. And if I did, it was for the better. I'm the same girl whose letters you tore up one day on the train. Only a little older. Even so, I think I'm prettier than I used to be. Am I wrong?

—No. You're not wrong.

She had a gold tooth. Her skin does not have the same glow; but her eyes do. Her hair is prettier, her breasts smaller, her waist more slender. Attractive, with something intense and ripe about her blue dress against the ochre wall and the black roof of the warehouse. Eudóxia is younger. But she looks older, in her frumpy dresses, with that absent and furtive air with which she disguises her suspicious nature. Every year her gait gets slower, her eyes more piercing, her mouth greedier. This one, on the contrary, has barely changed. Paper and pencil, colors. Fantasies. She was always like that, a dreamer. Now, by dint of dreaming, she is going to Granada. She was right when she used to say to me: "Some day we will travel, I know." We will. I look at the ships in the docks, it is all I have left of the adventures we longed for. To think that her life and mine one day followed the same course! We would be unhappy, this trip to Spain, never taken, would embitter our life together. Spain would exist in her mind as another destiny, a better one, perhaps, but forbidden, and therefore more desirable. She would never mention it, that is the worst of it, she would put the dream and the secret between us. No, thanks. Since she is a woman capable of conjuring up fantasies and giving them existence, let her devote her life to scrawling on paper. Cashews, birds, clowns. Will she send me the colorful postcard with the Gypsy dancers of Granada? If she does, she will not put her name on it: she is a sensible woman, after all. I can rest assured.

She smiles, her gold tooth gleaming in the light of the street lamp filtering through the branches of the *ficus*; he and the girl look as if they were caught in a net woven of shards of light and shade. With one gesture of her hand she takes in the deserted street, the wet sidewalks, the smell of damp earth enveloping them, the dogs barking, the closed doors and windows, the black sky. He, arms crossed, without a tie, his collar turned up, his body ill at ease in the clothes still new but already too short for his arms and legs, which are getting longer; she with bangs, her dress bunched at the waist, the full skirt making her still undefined hips look wider. She smells of powder, eau de cologne and clean laundry. Ashamed of his own voice, whose inflections he does not always recognize and which rarely obeys him even if he tries to modulate it (much less when, as a little while ago, he talks a lot or gets excited), he decides to shut up and listen to his girlfriend.

—You're right, I, too, think this town is miserable. When I read the papers from Recife and see all the things happening there, I get sad. Ocean liners, princes, movie actors arrive, there's an airport, a zoo, a public library, lots of movie theaters, military parades, trolleys, a river crossing the city, tall buildings. Paved streets. And the streetlights are so different. Here: railroad tracks, painted black. There: round, ornate, the color of silver, with the Republic's coat of arms. There are public gardens, full of benches. Imagine the biggest cities, Paris, Singapore, Manchester. If I were a man, I'd join the navy. Tell me this isn't a prison: we have to spend our entire life here, in this place. But who knows, maybe we'll take our journey, one day, across the sea.

We will. She says *we will.* But I, not you, will take this journey. Don't you know what a poet said to his sweetheart, who was probably like you and thought she would be with him forever? "I am Goethe!" I am somebody too, I will be famous, I feel that strength in me. Comfort, my father's money, family, hometown, I will leave it all behind. What I am destined to conquer I do not know yet. But I know that one day I will come back, crowned with glory. You will be married to a salesman, or maybe a clerk, you will have a home and children; but your greatest and unconfessed source of pride will be to have been what you are now: the witness to my adolescence. I am Goethe.

Everybody around the table, beneath the lamps filled with candles, listening to the priest's rhetoric, the sentences uttered so many times, on identical occasions, on fidelity, fervor, and the wedding of Cana. In the center of the embroidered tablecloth, set with English china and shining silverware, on top of the huge frosted cake, vaguely reminiscent of a Babylonian temple, two little dolls, representing the bride and the groom, hold a heart with the word LOVE written on it with silver powder. The ladies' faces, topped by hats of sundry origin faded with time and resuscitated with a bow or velvet flowers, are enraptured; the girls'—some are wearing stockings and high heels for the first time—quiver with anticipation; the men's affect gravity and circumspection, barely dissimulating (in their eyes, at the corners of their mouths) a certain expression of irony and tedium. Above the indistinct cloud of hats and faces, the father's face stands out, still bearing traces of his exultation at the realization of the alliance he has planned and arranged with skilled obstinacy; but already fading, annoyed as he is at the priest, who has been talking forever, belaboring the same old concepts, illustrating them with the same trite images.

Everybody, with this attentive air, these new clothes, is keeping in check the impulse to rush into the buffet and eat and drink proportionately to the value of the presents they sent: useless, tacky presents that will clutter the house, and that I will have to get rid of little by little, against Eudóxia's will, who never likes the idea of giving up any possession, even insignificant ones. The priest is the only one paying attention to his sermon, matching in length the importance of our families and the amount of the donation. These words of his, I know which way they flow. They do not ooze out through the door or the windows; they disappear at my side, forever, swallowed by this bottomless well to which I have tied my life and whose bony elbows are jabbing my side. With no enthusiasm for anything, no friends, indifferent to anything that does not increase her already large fortune, she swallows everything and nothing satiates her. She never returns or gives anything, ever, to anyone. As the years go by I will gradually get used to her furtive ways, her unremitting diffidence; and at the cost of seeing her succumb to aimless ambitions, I will end up by becoming her slave, moved by a compassion that should be directed to myself instead.

Why, then, these pious sentences, why talk of eternity and sacredness? We have joined two fortunes—and two poverties. That is all. It is the gold, it is the real estate that is sacred for us. If love does not unite us—and there is no love between us—how could it be eternal? And don't waste your time looking for symbols. For us only one holds, these vacuous puppets, flaunting a serious word (the word, the word!) on a paper heart. Probably I will not even be able to get rid of the presents we received today.

He waited until the employees had left to open the drawer, turn over the discolored folders, look for the papers. Would he remember them if it had not been for the news in the afternoon paper, the photographs of the paintings—exotic fruits, an extravagant bird—and the once familiar name? In the empty warehouse, with the anxiety of someone looking for a revealing document among many others, he finally found them. Here they are, the same eyes that beheld them, examining the visions expressed in those poems without recognizing them.

Poems. Why do I still keep them, after so many years? They're my poems; in any case, they are not unbearable, and a certain generosity, a certain feverishness flits through them. My heart was not pure, though; I admit that by then many of the repulsive creatures that my father's zeal nourished and that today make of me a dismal vivarium, already lived in it. Had it been otherwise, I would not have shown her these poems with such disdain, condescension and pride. I remember how slowly she read them. I thought it was because she did not understand them, when actually her lingering look was sounding their depth. She read my verses closely, she was glad for them, believed in me. And it wasn't me who finally broke out of the shell, discovering a creative and free way of living.

She trained the hands of her youth so that they would belong to her. As for me—these hands, cautious, almost always clenched, I do not know what subtle and laborious process molded them—in what recess of time, in what thick night of interrogatives did I lose mine?

A Point in the Circle

☐ No woman, until yesterday, had ever let her hair down for me. I remember when, as a boy, I heard a horn concert, an instrument I believed destined to a secondary role in the orchestra. Now, I try to imagine the elaborate arrangements in vogue in other times, a century and a half ago, for example. Back then—for receptions in villas surrounded by gardens, with limestone doorposts and sashes, rides in sedans carried by singing slaves, Mass in churches whose domes were covered with white and blue tiles, and even for the idle days at home—women arranged their hair with countless pins, flowers, combs and bodkins, and covered it with lace or gauze mantillas. They let it down, with a languid and sinuous gesture, when the doors of the dressing room closed and they removed from their arms, their necks, earrings, colored ribbons and gold chains before taking off their shoes, which were never black. Thus each of them was two different women: one whose hair was fastened up, visible to the world; and one with loose hair, the undulating movement of which imitated that of her shoulders and the folds of her billowing

41

nightgown. Their hair was a secret revealed to one man alone. If the intruder (I do not know her name and I did not ask her to come back) had not let down that mass of hair, shiny silk cords brushing against her waist, what other gesture could have been as significant an expression of intimacy and offering? I have seen many things in this boardinghouse, once the home of some rich merchant, in whose garden—its boundaries marked by a hedge of inter-woven palm leaves—clematis, China roses and passion flowers bloomed. But I will never see anything like yesterday again.

▽ On the tenth step, I realized it was the wrong address. I climbed the rest of the stairs and entered the room without closing the door behind me. Its occupant watches me from the wooden bed. Without paying attention to his uneven gaze, I lean forward slightly, arms behind my back, the wicker basket with the purple ribbon hanging from my left wrist, while I examine the painting on the wall. The occupant gets up without saying a word. Standing next to each other, we look as if we were at an exhibition, about to express an opinion on the model's hairdo or clothes. We do not. To get a better view of the drawing, a more global one, to unveil it, I take a step back. The door I really entered from was this picture, this woman whose spray of flowers I'd like to hold between my fingers. Enclosed in her dark frame, in profile, in a 17th-century costume, reminiscent of Anne of Austria in her dress and demeanor, she is holding—in a regal and delicate manner—the vertical spray with a single flower open at eye level. In some ways I would like to be like this girl, and gently hold, year after year, I too within a frame, my evergreen spray, its immortal corolla. As I examine the figure more closely I become convinced of it: our hands are alike. Mine do not feel heavy, when at rest; in motion, they never stumble over things, accomplishing everything with simple and skillful gestures.

☐ She looked around the room, like someone who tries to evoke, at a historical site, the events that made it famous. On the chair, in a glass, I had placed two carnations, now withering. She put the basket down next to the glass and rested her right hand on the back of the chair; the other was hanging at her side. She had torn from a carnation, with her equine teeth, the petal that she was now holding between her lips. This was the time to close the door, slowly. How long did we stand, facing each other, the visitor with her hands behind her back, perhaps her favorite posture? Was I standing between her and an imaginary being, for whom, with precise gestures, she had let her hair down? I felt like I was inside the picture, taken by the same sudden admiration with which she had leaned toward it earlier. It is because of this, and also for having become absorbed in the contemplation of its lines, that our gaze seems so lingering to me. Now, like those archeologists who think they'll reconstruct new birds and the trajectory of their flight thanks to a piece of wing found in a rock, I could compose for the stranger a whole world, starting from the fragment left in this room.

▽ Simplification does not mean lack of ornament. I am wearing a pearl-gray skirt and a green print blouse with black rhododendrons. My earrings are also black, to match the flowers on the fabric; a silver spiral bracelet; sandals with arabesques. My slip is white, rigorously starched, of cretonne with a wide pink ribbon threaded through the embroidery at the hem. In addition, the movements and even the pauses of my fingers acquire an ornamental function, like anything imprinted with the essentiality of those bulls finely engraved with sedge brushes on papyrus scrolls. I am tall and angular; you can see in me the long lines, flexible and firm, like the lines of a fencing foil, supporting the flesh. As for my life, I try to make a circle of it and find the Point, situated in the triangle and the square, a point mentioned by the stonecutters of the gothic period, who were convinced that without such knowledge all attempts at logic and harmony would be vain. That is why I rejoice when I realize that the man, whom I am now facing for the first time, has a glass eye. Glass eyes are not destined, like real ones, to see the ephemeral aspect of things. They imitate the organic world and fill the void with their neuter and specific existence. The perfection of such fragile objects lies in their technical rigor, in their adjustment to the living tissue, in the absence of asperities, in their discreet gleam and, above all, in not seeing. Those who regret the blindness of such artifacts are therefore wrong, forgetting as they do that they were not made to see and be corruptible. Glass eyes are abstract contemplators of eternity.

Maybe, then, my geometrical side will not be lost in this man's presence.

☐ Obliged, in order to earn some money, to play the saxophone from nine thirty to four in the morning even though my instrument has always been the oboe, I never spend the night at the boardinghouse. In the morning, I get off work, glance toward the old section of Recife, where the fortifications, the Navy arsenal and the warehouses used to be, picture the size and whiteness of the plantation-era buildings, cross the Maurício de Nassau bridge, cool my lips in the breeze coming up from the Capibaribe, cross Rua Nova, the Boa Vista bridge, Rua da Imperatriz, walking on the pavement that used to be made of red granite or bluish beach pebbles, reach my room on Gervásio Pires at daybreak. If it is raining, I wait until it stops; I never take the bus. I drink coffee, lie down. I go downstairs at mealtimes, chat for a while in the dining room, where the floor used to be covered with carpets, and the walls hung with English prints of hunting scenes. Where would the Broadwood piano have been? I go back to bed and, if I am not sleepy, I lie still, hours and hours, not even dreaming of playing the oboe, my hands at my sides, palms up, watching the spiders at work on the ceiling. They stretch their webs between one rafter and the other; thread by thread, with unfailing movements, they establish links that the wind or a beetle could destroy, they weave their transparent threads one after the other, they weave a force between the rafters.

☐ Since I arrived, four years ago, the boarding house

has already passed through the hands of three different owners: a pair of dentists, the lieutenant, the Spanish widow. They all refused to put a window in here, no matter how small. The two rectangles on the ceiling, of opaque bluish-green glass, six feet apart, the ridgepole between them, is what makes this room inhabitable. And if they do not cool it off, they at least let some light in, even on rainy days. At the beginning of the last century, the space now occupied by the table, the painting, the oboe next to the music sheets, the blue urinal and the armoire with suitcases on top was filled with the large pans, the copper pots and the stove. The kitchen was always on the upper floor. It is unlikely that the dining room would have been in the same place where we eat now: since the ground floor was almost always left for the blacks' quarters and the stables, the piano, the English prints and the carpets must have been somewhere on the first floor. Wearing slippers and long gowns, their breasts almost hanging out, the Misses wandered from the ground floor to the kitchen, yelling at the slaves, eating plates of sweets and yawning. They rarely wore their best clothes at home, and certainly very few bathed at night. They wore gold ornaments, bright-colored capes, ribbons in their hair only when they went out. It is also unlikely that there would have been roses and clematis in this garden, so near the horses. Passion vines, yes, it is possible; and perhaps floss-silktrees, lemons, a few tamarinds. Today it is a cement patio, with caladiums growing out of cans, cacti and maidenhair. The cat was snoozing among them. The clangor of noon over—locks, bells, hinges, silverware and latches—silence had fallen, the afternoon pause. The guests of the boarding house were taking a nap; locked up in her room, the Spanish woman was fanning herself with her tortoise shell fan, her dress hiked up to her thighs. This summer calm heightens my senses, yet numbs my grasp of reality. This is why, even though I had not heard anything—no steps, no voice—I was convinced there was someone in the room, someone barefoot or wearing light shoes, and I was not surprised.

▽ He closed the door, carelessly; I began to unbutton my blouse. Five thousand years ago many insects, birds, fish, plants and quadrupeds inhabited the Nile and its banks. The signs that joined them and transformed them, forcing them into rigorous constraints contrary to their mutable nature, did not expect them to fly, or swim, or sing, or blossom on stone and papyrus. They merely reduced them to luminous syntheses, stripping them of what was accessory. This was their goal. If they, the Egyptians, knew the joy of writing, it is because they had found—a rare occurrence—the balance between life and rigor, between disorder and geometry. On our knees, silent, profile against profile, we look like dolls cut out of a doubled sheet of paper—silhouettes that, only apparently in opposition, complete each other, constitute the same unity, unfolded; or the patronesses of High Egypt and the Delta, goddesses adorning the kings' foreheads, one with a white crown, the other with a blood-red one, representing the south and the north of the country who, together, were

47

given a name by which they merged into one—a name unrelated to their previous designations. Where will they be, in the multiple, varied and excessive being I recognize in myself, those exact profiles—of vulture or winged serpent—discovered by the scribes of the Nile?

☐ My face pressed against the pillow, I pictured myself lying on the beach and remembered her hair, strewn here only a few minutes earlier. My desire was slowly coming back. I had the impulse to turn, to stop the visitor, I dared not move or speak. I could hear her moving away from me, this time definitively, putting the pins in her hair, her clothes, and an undefinable rigidity of gestures between us. Before we came, together, to bed, I carried her to the center of the room; I wanted to see the tone and texture of her skin in the light. I noticed that the sun had disappeared and heard the rain, soft, falling on the rooftiles. From her deep breathing I thought that she, too, was listening at the same instant, suspended in my arms, to the sound that had escaped me. After she left, slamming the door, without having said a single word to me, not even good-bye, I lazily turned my head. The rain had passed, a sunbeam was climbing up the armoire. How many times would it cover that trajectory before I died?

▽ It was in the Gulf of Mexico, in 1924, a little over forty years ago. A hurricane swept the coast of Florida, Alabama, Mississippi, reached Louisiana, yanked out trees, roofs and telegraph lines. No matter how fast the terrestrial animals crawled, ran or flew, the water and the wind were faster. Not much was left of the big herds: in a few seconds 250,000 cattle and horses were dead. Almost all the reptiles, amphibians, waterfowl, almost all the fish living in the lakes and lagoons suffered an identical fate. Washed onto the beach, the corpses were buried in an immense shroud of alluvion and debris, carried by the waves. They will remain there many years; some will be rediscovered one day, turned into stone. I am barefoot.

☐ Her naked body, her strewn hair. Her long arms crossed on the pillow, the nervures of her wrists, half hidden in her black hair, were throbbing. I looked at the hair under her armpits, tawny, damp. It gave off a resinous smell, of raw chestnuts. Two straight lines, traced between them and the shadow of her bellybutton, would both touch the rosettes of her large breasts. The invisible stems of these sunflowers met, below her belly, in the narrow vase of her pubis. Her left thigh, stretched out, lay on top of the other. The suppleness of her skin, its warmth, the throbbing of her muscles and the discolored down, halfway up her thighs, mitigated the hardness that had disappointed me in the shape of her legs, in her bony and rough-skinned knees and in her veiny feet. With the rain, the light in the dirty skylights—dark varnish—stained our bodies.

☐ There was a moment when she stood in front of me—so near that, if we had stretched out our arms, we would have touched. Without knowing it, without wanting it, she had come to meet me and here she was, surrendering to her determination as if it were her destiny.

Seated, my head down, my hands clutching the sheet, I saw that she had taken her sandals off. An invisible spider, diligently weaving, was bringing us together. We would not speak, of that I was sure. We both obeyed laws unknown to us and our tongues were tied, so that everything would happen with precision and in silence. A dance.

▽ We are two bodies, we are one body. The real eye sees at a glance my asperities, my imperfection, what in me is unfinished and thus contiguous to its nature. Meanwhile, before the other pupil, as alien as before the universe of the young woman who resembles Anne of Austria, my mortal side dissolves. I turn into a dual entity, visible to a human eye and redeemed by an artificial one in its cold and lucid hardness. For this, I am the Great Celestial Cow, the goddess of love, joy, music, dance and garland weaving. Then, after we part again, I will throw my right leg over his and draw on his shoulder, with the tip of my breast, as if it were spilling out milk or blood, the sun, thick braids, perfect triangles, horns, the pentagram, symbol of life.

□ To take off her pleated skirt, to unbutton her linen blouse (her right hand was casually moving down the small mother-of-pearl buttons), she did not take her eyes off me. Despite this, she seemed not to see me. Her breasts, naked, were larger than I had imagined. Ecstatic, my arms outstretched, I took them in my hands and lifted them slightly, in an attitude of offering and acceptance. Strange weight and strange consistency: docile, fugitive, liquid, almost impalpable. Bent backwards, her long legs flexed, a collapsing arc resting on my right arm, which firmly holds her swaying waist, she took my lower lip between her teeth; with my left hand buried in her hair, which brushed the floor like a horse's tail, I held her head. A curved line, opaque, overlaying another of identical thickness, but taking on, in my mind, the transparency of a rainbow, this is what I was. Our desire, making us lighter and increasing our strength, balanced us.

▽ Just as the horses, cows, amphibians, fish and waterfowl wait underground, in the Gulf of Mexico, for the passing of time and some event that will reveal to us their petrified effigies, the other animals remained in the papyrus scrolls covered by the sands of the desert, protected by the dry climate, while above them the soldiers of Ethiopia, Assyrians, Persians, Greeks, Romans, and many more, nameless, passed and disappeared, leaving no trace. Life and memory work in the same way, subverting with equal indifference the pure and the impure, not letting them surface ever again, or until man's works, or chance, make it possible. In a little while, I will go downstairs, cross the hall where nobody will see me, go out in the street. I will be holding between my fingers geometric flowers and my dress will be like Anne of Austria's. And then? What armies, sands and debris will cover this hour? Today, tomorrow, buried or not, evoked or forgotten, I refuse to exist only in my rigor; or only in my disorder. Let this moment be, and my existence with it, the geometrician's angles and the animals of the hurricane.

☐ Her face, suddenly pale, framed by her thick and

disheveled hair, glowed like an opal. Was it made of cedar? What beauty did it conceal? Mongolian face, unfinished, sculpted by someone who wanted to force a mark of sadness on the wood, without having the strength to suppress the triumphant joy latent in the model which, rebelliously, had prevailed on the material. Thick, flat lips, without prominence, parted because of the heat, lust and the size of her teeth. She did not try to mask their indefinite contour by painting them. The slant of her dark eyes, almost black and at that moment liquid with pleasure, was accentuated with pencil. They stared at me with fervor or gratitude, as if they had been waiting for me forever. I thought of myself as her ground and roots. Soon I would fall down exhausted, my body would fall down, while I myself would remain—how I do not know—fastened to her. We were joined, entwined. The villas that graced the banks of the Capibaribe, white, with their limestone window sashes and their orchards, did not exist anymore; the snow-white plantation-era buildings and the red granite pavement were also gone; and there were not any more churches with domes covered with white and blue porcelain tiles. A tormented hymn rose from us, from our glistening skin, the remembrance of the horn and its possibilities fleeted through my consciousness, we both breathed hard with pleasure. So many things changed—architecture, systems of government, clothing, customs, the forms of misery and covetousness—so many things changed and the hymn was the same.

Hahn's Pentagon

¶ IN DIFFERENT TOWNS, ⊦ I here in Goiana, ¶ I in Vitória, ⊱ we go to see Hahn's number, and these two shows ¶ were, ⊦ are ⊱ identical, because everything takes place with the regularity of repeated rehearsals. ¶ I used to have, have always had, a predilection for this kind of animal; even though I was already forty-five, I was still thrilled when I saw them. I was fascinated by that formless being engraved on cave walls when the destiny of humanity was still uncertain, minter's die, transportation of kings, mount of gods, revered and believed to be the animal that bears the world on its back. Besides, knowing this was a race approaching extinction affected me deeply, perhaps because I am a bachelor. Miss Hahn entered to the sound of *Aida*'s Triumphal March.⊱ A crimson rug on her forehead, Persian carpets on her back, ¶ she appeared, ⊦ looms, ⊱ her ears fanning, her tusks sparkling in the limelight; ¶ she danced, ⊦ dances, ¶ with her trainer, ⊦ with the great general, a waltz, ⊱ passages from *The Blue Danube*, ¶ she joined ⊦ joins ¶ drew together ⊱ her legs on two colored drums, lifting her trunk and turning slowly, with great caution, on that minuscule pedestal,¶ where she drank, ▸ where she drinks ¶ where she had ⸾ a glass of beer; ¶ she bestowed, ▸ gives, ¶ offered, ⸾ to someone seated in the first row , ¶ a bunch of dahlias, ▸ three yellow roses; ¶ she left, ▸ goes away, ¶ disappeared, ⸾ gently stepping on the ground; ¶ you had ▸ I have, ⸾ the impression that if she found an egg in her path ¶ she would remain ▸ will remain ¶ would remain ⸾ suspended in the air not to break it. ▸ In my nightmare, I open the window: its entire space is filled with a dark gray mass, wrinkled and swaying. A wall erected in secret, dissolving, threatening to invade the sill, the room, to bury me? I cry out: "Hahn!" Adélia hears me screaming, takes me in her arms.

‖ Busy with our elderly brother, the priest, who was sick at the time, I found out about the show from Nassi Latif. I did not even get to see the elephant, even though the house where we live is, so to speak, in the same court-yard in which she used to spend mornings and after-noons; it was so near that my sister and I heard her bel-lows all day long. In the beginning I would invite Helônia to go see her with me after we cleaned up the house. She had not gone out with me for a long time, she said that two old women in the street, strolling together, were ri-diculous, and maybe she had a point there, but not much of one. Were we so old? She was not even seventy, I was barely sixty-three. There are people who get married at this age, and she herself was planning to marry Nassi. Nassi would go to the Circus—I do not know how he got the money—and the following day he would show up, crazy as ever, telling the same things in great detail, as if he had not already told my sister and me many other times. Helônia, even though she denied it, adored him: she never left him, listening to him, asking questions, eating him up with her eyes. Out of compassion, she said. I would leave them to look after our sick brother. This one, now, he was old. Deaf, almost blind, he could not even hear the elephant's bellows (God bless him) and it is hard to imagine what would have become of him without the assistance of sisters like us, still in our prime and ready to do anything to help him. As soon as Latif left (Helônia used to walk him to the gate) the argument would start. My sister, however much I tried to open her eyes, refused to understand that those daily calls were not proper: Nassi Latif was not a boy, but a thirty-some-year-old man, an irresponsible crazy bum, who could easily compromise us, two defenseless women, whose only riches were our brother the priest, the family name, our reputation and our virginity, these two precious in themselves, mainly because of the zeal with which we had guarded them for over half a century.

⚔ Pushing out my bust as much as I can and lifting my nephew at the same time (he is six, five years younger than my breasts), here I am in Hahn's presence, in a light brown dress, looking at her teats, small like her eyes with their light-colored lashes, teary, dark gray butterflies, nibbled at—but not killed—by clothes moths and ants. The night has fallen in the elephant's belly. Those of us who are standing around her, offering her lumps of salt, sugar-coated almonds, candy, sugar cane and pieces of indigo, will soon leave the still sunny courtyard and go home. If only the afternoon were longer! If only I could stay among the high school boys longer, if they could all see me in this dress. Not that it is new; but, even though I am not blond and pretty like Patricia Lane, Marjorie Reynolds or Carole Lombard, my main asset is my breasts—large, firm—and the blouse enhances them. This is the beginning of important events in my monotonous life. I am not aware that I am being carried, alone, by the current (my nephew did not fall into these waters) and I look at Hahn. Her joyfulness goes beyond the festive circle of schoolboys, old people, housewives, vendors, it spills onto the sun-drenched courtyard, as if she were not a dull and rather unspectacular animal, but a band, or fireworks. Her huge ears, like dirty old rags, streaked with gold, off-white and faded pink—bouquets of wilted flowers, of putrescence and dust—flap above the crowd, making me think of streamers, knights' crests, ribbons and flags. Her hide is the somber color of old iron; through some play of light, it gives off a glaucous hue, like the sea. It is only then that I see Bartolomeu's eyes, also liquid, but blue, and think they must be the source of the inexplicable marine tones softening the elephant's loins, and I myself feel, for an instant, bathed in blue. He must be, at most, twelve or thirteen. Perplexity, fascination and doubt do not cloud my judgment. We are equal in height.

⊖ I have not come to town for almost two months. Seized by a sudden desire to see again the shops and groceries open for business, the barber shop where I went during my adolescence and the schoolboys carrying books under their arms, heading for the school where I studied, all things I have not seen for a long time, since I only come to town on Sundays (and also, it is possible, because I dreaded the idea of spending these two days at home—tomorrow is a holiday in Recife—enduring the most unpleasant presence of all, that of someone we no longer love), I left after lunch, giving my wife a quick kiss on her cheek, since, despite the growing distance between us, we still maintain these small dead rituals, so painful. If I had come by train, I would not have seen the elephant: the route between the station and my grandmother's house does not pass by the church plaza; coming by bus, though, I get off in front of the circus. So I see Miss Hahn, at one in the afternoon, in the shade of the awning, like one of those oriental potentates of the movies, in the midst of all that sun, privileged characters lying among cushions, as proud of their square of shade as of their daggers and cool emeralds. An old man is looking at her. The two of them are alone, alone in the shade, amidst the torrid silence, and Hahn is holding one leg up in the air; she is performing an endless dance, a to and fro motion to which her weight itself, her largeness, impart grace, a solemn rhythm. She is an Asian specimen: she has five nails in her front feet, four in the back. The end of her tail looks like a peacock feather. The old man asked me if I did not think it cruel to capture an animal, isolate it from its companions, train it with baths, chants, deceitful rewards, shouts, all for money. I smiled without answering. How could I agree, I who believe that undomesticated words, loose in limbo, alone or in packs, in a wild state, are useless angelic powers? With a sinuous movement Hahn has uncoiled her trunk: she is blowing between my fingers.

¶ At the office, colder and emptier than my bachelor's life, I could not stop thinking about Miss Hahn. I have two brothers, very different from one another, and perhaps I am a mix of the two, the midway point between them. The elder, Oséas, had a good shoe store, in which the other, Armando, was a partner. In this capacity he showed up two or three times a week, slunk away among the shelves or stood at the door, ethereal eyes, always dressed in white, hands in his pants pockets, and then, from a certain point on, in his coat pockets, because that was what George Raft did in a movie. Suddenly, without saying good-bye to Oséas, he would calmly head home, pass by my office without turning his head, and go back to his colors and brushes in the solitude of his studio, to paint saints, Scandinavian landscapes and animals he had never seen: hippopotamus, herons, whales, sharks. Oséas, when he was a little over twenty, took a wife. Without great pretensions, taking into account only her teeth (an unequivocal sign, according to him, of good or bad health) and the slenderness of her legs. He thought women with big legs tended to be lazy. He liked fishing, ate well and heartily, drank even more, and always kept several dozen bottles of wine at home, indifferent to their labels and origin. "It's all wine!" He hated sadness, and only went to see films with pleasant titles: *Long Live the Navy, The Captain's Daughter, Delicious, Youth Rules.* This was the weak point in the sound construction he affected to be, the false note that gave him away: my brother, a man afraid like the rest of us, looking at life askance. A man cannot call himself brave, eager to live, if he is not capable of looking the terrible in the eye, wherever it may be. He could not stand it when prostitutes (he continued to go to them even after his marriage) told him about their problems. "A whore's born a whore. They're all worthless." He was the least inclined to subtlety of any creature I ever knew. Without ever having cultivated this virtue, without possessing it in the least bit, my life became entangled in distinctions and details, not blind enough to bite off and chew what I hungered for or crazy enough to enter a dream and become part of it. If the girls of this town did not seem romantic enough to kindle a passion in me, and if I never conceived of a marriage unglorified by the exaltation, illusory as it may be, of senses and soul, casual relationships repulsed me. I also had more than enough sense of reality, which prevented me from transcending the trivial and the petty by means of the imagination, as well as singling out a nonexistent being, bringing forth like Adam a woman from my own entrails, immaculate, perfect, invulnerable—and loving, with true love, this imaginary character. So, almost every night, after work, I wandered the streets alone, no longer knowing how many years (how many?) it had been since I had felt a woman's body against mine, thinking about leaving, knowing I would never do it, longing for the impossible and sudden appearance, in one of those out-of-the-way streets enveloped in squalor, of the woman who would come to my rescue, freeing from its solitude, if only for one day, this soul of mine, filled with the silence of courtyards before daybreak.

‖ Our solitude—my sister's, our brother the priest's, mine—was also great. I can affirm that not all saints were as virtuous as him. Maybe it was precisely because of this that, even though he had practiced the ministry for thirty-nine years in this town, baptizing, celebrating weddings, commending the souls of the dead to God and organizing processions, almost no one came to see him. So it is understandable that, even though I feared the consequences of Nassi's daily calls and did not like his ways very much, I looked forward to them and became anxious if he happened to be late. It is also easy to explain the fact that, two weeks after the elephant's arrival, I, who had heard so much about her ways, began to experience a strange feeling, a sense of joy, when the sound of her trumpet filled the air. I had the impression that she was calling me; I began to answer those cries, feeling guilty if I did not.

↙ The sacristy in the dark. The priest on the high altar, the two altar boys, candles burning, the gold of the images, white embroidered cloths, the red carpet. The sacred hymn, sung in Latin. The old organ. The moonlight comes in through the window that opens onto a yard with mango trees; it reflects on the mosaic floor, shines on the dark wooden pews. Bartolomeu beside me, erect, hands in his pockets. Five days passed before he found the courage to talk to me. Today he followed me resolutely, matching his step with mine, a little faster or longer. I let him get close. I walked faster when I sensed that he was on the verge of the decision I yearned for. We entered the church almost at the same time and I guessed—more than heard—his strangled voice, asking if we could talk. Without looking at him, feeling nervous too, despite myself, I said yes. The hymn, the priest's voice, the sound of the bell, the moonlight in the sacristy. I am standing a little bit in front of Bartolomeu; from time to time I look at him. He responds with his bashful and courteous smile. I know: his soul is not hollow. And, from this first contact on, I have the presentiment that something out of the ordinary is awaiting me. What's brewing in the secret of his fragile body (which gives me the almost obsessive impression of some rare piece of clockwork in a watchmaker's shop)? It is like peering through the dark at a plot of land where vague movements indicate to us an unfolding of intentions, an attack, an escape, a conspiracy, something whose nature and purpose we do not know. This child scares me.

⊖ My grandmother's house, door and window, fifteen feet across the front. The distribution of the rooms, in keeping with the plan local designers and builders have been copying for years—front room, a corridor along the bedrooms, dining room, kitchen, bathroom, yard—gives it the appearance of an old house. It was built less than

ten years ago, and the quality of the materials is inferior
to those used for older houses. No stone, no ornamental
tiles, no pinecones on the eaves, no cedarwood or metal
latticework. It is not even very tall. On the right, in a
separate cottage, lives her married daughter, whom she
goes to see every day and who, not being very fond of
going out, finds this ritual, always reciprocated, a diver-
sion. Closed doors, everybody is taking a siesta. I pushed
open the cottage's little gate, crossed the porch. My grandmother had left the kitchen door open in her house. Due
to the unevenness of the terrain her side of the wall is
lower. I took a ladder (no oriental would dare get on the
back of an elephant by such a vulgar device), climbed
the wall without any difficulty, I am inside the clean silent
house, among the china closets, the split-cane chairs and
the bare table, square, all of white wood. My grandmother's presence pervades the smell of things. On the
way from the yard to this dining room I have been grinding the elephant's breath between my fingers, as if it were
hot, damp sand. I realize, for the first time, how sterile my
life has become and how hostile the environment in which
the better part of my days is spent. A monster, beneath
the sun and amidst the silence; a pachyderm, not in size,
but for my aridity and inner poverty; with the aggravat-
ing circumstance that everything in me is secret and does
not elicit the curiosity of others, not even accidentally;
and with the attenuating circumstance that I am not mute,
I have the word at my disposal, an instrument I handle
poorly, but I could train myself to record, if not my exile,

my perseverance in trying to break out of it. Here, among this furniture, I realize that seeing the town again on a Monday is an excuse. If it has been long since I have found in these monthly visits to my grandmother's a certain undefinable flavor, which, I am sure, existed in my childhood, I imagine—with the logic of the destitute—that this flavor, or this atmosphere, has moved from Sunday to some other day. A coward's excuses.

⸖ The street where we live is one of the oldest in town. Its level has risen with the years; or the rudimentary brick sidewalk, almost buried, has given little by little, as time goes by: the street proper and the sidewalk blend together. What month is it? End of August? Beginning of September? The sky littered with restless kites. Other boys fly them, all day long, on the street of the buried sidewalks. Across from our house lives a woman. She makes up for everything old and without charm. Her name is Adélia. In the morning, after her husband, a cereal merchant, goes to work, she leans out of the green window. At the same time, I, on my tiptoes, lean out of mine. She nods, smiles, lets herself be adored by someone she thinks is just an innocent boy. Aware of my envy—I would get sunburnt watching the buzzing antelopes, the imposing Indians and the stingrays soaring in the sky: rectangular, nervous, menacing, with sharp pieces of glass at the end of their tails—she brought me from the market, among oranges, lettuce hearts and bananas, this ruby red Indian, palpitating in the porter's basket, this Indian whose strength I sense with pride. I had to fight the grown-ups' opposition at home: they say that kites carry the smallpox virus present in the upper atmosphere. They seem to be right, I myself have seen it; it is always in October, after the kites, that people in town develop smallpox, fever and other diseases. How did Adélia guess that of all kites I prefer the Indian, the Indian, a big square of color with one corner pointing down and the chain of tissue paper hanging from its sides enhancing, as it happens with kings' crowns, its splendor while increasing its stability? Leaning out of the window, Adélia smiles. A brief smile, short-lived, like all my joys. After sending my red Indian two or three *messages* (by what miracle do the small paper wheels reach the kite's bridle?), the curved taut string will snap, the Indian, vacillating, will get caught in the chain of tissue paper, the round messages will fly away with him. I will never see him again.

‖ Helônia and I had several arguments. "You're becoming too attached to Latif!" She insulted me: she was of age and would do whatever she wanted with her life. We bear the same name, I answered, your mistakes fall upon me. She burst into tears, saying that she was unhappy, and screamed that I was jealous. Nassi Latif was the last person who could arouse my jealousy, I declared. A madman. A tramp. I told her not to kid herself. Even with one side of his body paralyzed he would be running like a blue streak any day, crutches and all, he would go off to Acre or Mato Grosso, to Venezuela, as he had done so many times before. He was born a tramp, had lived like a tramp until then, and he would grow old and

66

die a tramp. She threw herself on the floor, wailing and kicking her feet. After this Nassi Latif did not come to see us for three days. Thinking that he had stopped coming because of me, because of my advice, a letter I had sent or something like that, she poisoned my food. When she saw me filling my plate, she repented, confessed to her wrong, knelt and asked me to forgive her. Our brother the priest knew nothing of what was going on.

✍ I know that the relationship between me and this boy cannot last; but I had hoped to see it die as a consequence of its own absurdity—a game in which someone agrees to be the King or the Wolf and takes on this role for a while. I realize now that the cruelty of people we have never wronged is turning against us, whose only crime is loving each other or trying to—dooming what is already transitory enough in itself to an even more premature end than that determined by its nature. It was my nephew who warned me about the whistling. Maybe Bartolomeu had heard it too; he did not say anything to me. He is tactful, even though he is just a boy. In the beginning, hoping that he would still be unaware of that inexplicable manifestation of the townspeople, I avoided meeting him in broad daylight. I looked for the darkest places. He did not take advantage, not once, of these circumstances: hands in his pockets, he looks at me furtively (his glances have something of the curious and frightened scrutiny of a little mouse venturing from its hiding place for a few seconds, but they shine with adoration), which delights me. A while ago, though, we do not know where it came from—some dark closed house, or behind a wall—the whistling began, *Aida*'s Triumphal March. Tactfully, without letting on that he heard it, he suggested that we go somewhere else. As I moved, I felt the fullness of my hips and realized that with a little malice a resemblance to Hahn can be found in my heavy walk, my swaying haunches, my waistless trunk. Even my breasts, of which I have always been so proud, looked huge to me. Our poor love, precarious and fragile, will drown in ridicule. We will be left with a humiliating memory of it all. That's why I look at the houses of this suddenly hateful town, before which I am Hahn and Bartolomeu my trainer, and I begin to cry. This is the first time he has taken my hand in his. I would like to give him a bunch of dahlias, as a sign of gratitude.

⊖ I look at the roof. What strange feeling has come over me? What mysterious space did I enter, jumping over the wall and invading this silent house in such an unusual way? My grandmother was sleeping, is sleeping, a sheet pulled over her legs. Her age no longer allows her to fill with her presence the entire house, with its nearly forgotten recesses and pieces of furniture, like this cot I cleaned, made up, lay down on, and which was covered with dust. Opening the big dresser drawer, taking out the sheets, the pillow, the pillowcase, the old pajamas, lying on the bed on my back. Banal gestures, permeated— why?— by a transcendent quality. My grandmother writes to me, the night of my nineteenth birthday: "I fixed a special meal. Your aunt and her husband, who are thinking about moving close to me because of my age, which unfortunately is quite advanced, came from the country. Since it was Sunday, we were sure you would come. We ate alone, at two in the afternoon, sad, because we had been looking forward to your visit for many weeks." Where was I that Sunday? A door, maybe the kitchen's, moves slowly, steadily, hits the jamb, the hinges creak, musically. Old noises, suspended in the silence of extinct summers. Need to cry. Vivid impression of being led, like a litter with religious images in a procession, toward something vague, but no less solemn because of this. Are all the currents of time flowing away simultaneously? Do dams, detours, stagnant periods of time by any chance exist, do certain hours return, incarnating themselves, by some kind of transmigration, in the substance of smells and noises, of light, of temperature, and enfolding us? The white elephant, because of its extreme rarity, was for a long time honored with homages, sacred candles, theatrical representations, rich regalia, jewels, processions. It was awesome. I, too, feel afraid at the presentiment of a dead time, huge and white, approaching me, or more than a time, gigantic blocks, a fleet of ghost ships, full of astrolabes, winds, compasses, the pattering of bare feet, heartbeats, deserted tables, three faces filled with vain expectation, holds with vats full of fresh water which I disdained before, looking for it in dry vats. Sails flapping, masts swaying, waves.

⅃ Among the kites gliding, serene, in the smallpox-infested air rose the Novelty, the Event. A famous pastoral play vies with Hahn for the interest of the public. (I go to a show with Adélia and her husband. In my left hand the woman's; in my right the grain seller's. To be able to endure this contact I have turned into a sack into which the man pours cereals and my friend various kinds of sugar—brown, white, crystallized—with bees and ants. On a tall wooden platform, lit by two large carbide lamps and round colored paper lanterns, the shepherdesses sing, heavily made up, ribbons in their hair, tambourines decorated with artificial flowers, red or blue boleros, with little gold medals and glass bead embroideries, very short skirts and long silk stockings, fastened at the thighs. They wear hoops in their ears and black beauty spots on their chins, foreheads or near their noses. Chains of crepe paper, also blue and scarlet, intersect above the bandstand, joining one lantern to the next. The orchestra: a fife, a banjo and a triangle. The audience is so loud that I can barely hear the instruments and the shepherdesses' hoarse voices). Anyway, the impresario thought up this festive way of announcing the show on the days the dancer-singers perform: at four thirty he lets loose a blue, blood-red and orange kite he made and which is not like the others, any other. It is huge, regal, snarling, has more than one surface, is full of festoons and resembles a fish, a hawk, an umbrella, a knick-knack case, a pinwheel. It fascinates me. I decide I will make a kite like that, with a new shape, different from the others and even brighter. I am going to make it.

¶ I closed the office early, went to Oséas' shop, invited

him to go see the enthusiastic crowd that, every afternoon, surrounded the tent where the elephant received
from the people, with the same graciousness, leafy
branches, honeyballs, lumps of salt, banana leaves, hand-
fuls of hay. He turned down my invitation and even asked
me if I thought he would leave the shop just to see an
animal. "If it were Ann Sheridan, maybe!" Armando also
refused to go with me:

—Too many people.

—You've already been there?

—No.

—Don't you like to paint animals?

—It's not a matter of liking. It's a necessity.

—But why don't you want to see an elephant up close?

—I don't need to. I know very well what an elephant
looks like.

—That's what you think. Which direction do the lines
on their back go? Lengthwise or from the top down?

—From the bottom to the top.

—Wrong. They have the shape of a small boat. They
look like a canoe, drawn in profile.

I left gnashing my teeth. It was absurd how I had retained certain traits typical of a twenty-year-old without
being able to find substitutes for them: the thin sideburns,
the way my coat's shoulders were cut, the habit of using
suspenders and even a certain way of walking down the
street—nonchalant, leisurely, hands behind my back, an
absent-minded look. I was aware that I was the only one
who still retained these characteristics, common to all el-

egant youths of my time; to change, however, was nearly impossible. Maybe, deep inside, I was proud of that loyalty which had turned me into a museum piece. Despite my anger towards my brothers, after the ridiculous discussion about the lines on the elephant's back, my gait was the same as ever. I had to affect the usual indifference, the usual serenity; nobody had the right to surmise my anger. Older people greeted me in a tone both respectful and condescending, as if there were something threatening and despicable about me: I was a serious man, but a confirmed bachelor. I went on, heading for the elephant's tent like someone going to see his girlfriend, like someone who has run away from home, disregarded the punishment, rebelled against oppression and is heading for the planned encounter, full of a love our parents do not understand and want to kill. Happy, I drew closer to Hahn. She was dancing as usual and the endless groups succeeded one another. She seemed to be laughing and was certainly exulting, the focus of that small and happy universe. When I saw her, the joy I felt vanished. Before the couples, the groups of girls, I suddenly felt like a character in some movie, or book, or nightmare, invisible in a world that was not mine and would never hear my voice. How could they hear me, if there were two decades between us, if I was hollering to them from far away, from the year 1930? I did not eat anything. I crossed the town, walked to the outskirts, got hungry, lost my appetite, headed for the red-light district.

✒ This is the last time we will see each other in public,

we did not say a word about it, but we know, it is the last time. I was the one who had the idea of meeting in the movie theatre, for the matinee of the Sabu movie. We arrived when there were still very few people and sat next to each other. In what way are we different from the others, to justify all these precautions? The theatre was full of couples, girls with boys, teen-agers, sweethearts. I was becoming more and more afraid of being with him, like someone who commits adultery, or is being watched by the police. Now I can see why: I was quite right. At first it was a distant whistling; which, timidly and then malevolently, was joined in by others, a swarm of angry wasps, repeating insistently, intermingled with belches, laughing, imitations of trumpetings, the March that for us was never triumphal but full of despair, accompanied by the rhythmical stomping of feet, fifty feet, three hundred, trampling over us. At first I tried to smile; then I had to make an effort not to cry. Without a word, Bartolomeu firmly grasped my hand and is still holding it, even though the whistling has ceased, not without a jeer or two. He is very pale; his lips, cracked and dry, look like a withered flower, petals without luxuriance. When the lights go out, I will leave. He will too, perhaps. We will not watch Sabu's movie, and possibly we will not see each other again, separated forever because of this sort of conspiracy, these whistles turned against us.

⊖ I do not know what woke me. I lie still, just listening at first, then I open my eyes. My grandmother and her daughter are talking in the living room. If I pay attention

I will know what they are talking about, the walls are thin, the house small, the door of my room is open. I let myself be lulled by the alternation of those voices, interrupted from time to time by short laughs. The sentences have the cadence of this town, and the conversation is the same one that has been going on for years, continuing during absences, repeating itself, going back to the beginning. At times they talk about old conversations they had. The sun is going down. Orange beams pierce the gaps between the roof tiles, illuminate spiderwebs lost among the rafters. A light breeze is also coming through the tiles; the spiderwebs sway gently, and so does the light in the room. My presentiment was true, then. I have entered the past, I am living simultaneously in this Sunday afternoon and in another distant time, ubiquitous, experiencing in time the state other men must have known in another dimension, in space. Would the same thing have happened if I had come in through the door? I know with certainty that I will never experience this again. I will be happy again. But now, among the thousands of possibilities of life, a space has opened up, a sphere, a lucky coincidence, a propitious configuration of factors, of great duration and amplitude: harmony between the moment I am immersed in and the deepest necessities of being. Eager to record everything, I wait, alert, for the interruption, the end. Watching for the new element (a door opening, a rooster crowing, a cloud covering the sun) which will forever undo this rare conjunction, I do not realize that this suspense disconnects me from my well-being, from the privileged center of this moment, since, even though I am still immobile, a mortal contraction is already present in me. And just when, engrossed in my ecstasy, I realize that my anticipation is among its causes, it actually begins to die, it fades away, without any possibility of subsisting, since my disenchantment, my emptiness, all the poisons that are replacing the sap of life are contained within the structure of happiness, and they are weakening me. So I drink with ardor this spectral resurgence of the past still lingering in the sound of voices, in the undulations of the light, in the spiderwebs.

⊦ I have been working on the kite for days. Or rather nights, after having done my grammar, geography, history and natural science homework. I have used up sticks, cans of glue, sheets and sheets of the tissue paper Adélia provides me with, I have drawn, imagined impossible sketches, cried. My imagination strays, despairs. Many years ago, the town used to have running water. With time, since the people did not know how to keep what was given to them, the pipes deteriorated and once again the supply was delivered on the back of a donkey. The houses are full of jugs inside which the water sleeps. Tiny minnows swim in the jugs; they eat mosquito nymphs. There are still vestiges of the old piping, which disappears underground, connected to mysterious springs: big faucets, green with verdigris, dried up, forever open into muddy cement tanks. Without anyone knowing why, these faucets will suddenly start dripping water. "The fountain has awakened," the grown-ups say. This gift, this water that does not cost us a penny, we who are poor, seems a miracle. It can last a short time; or a long one, entire nights, never entire days, the fountain likes vigils. Granted in the same miraculous way, tonight the kite was born in my mind, with its framework of lines, surfaces and other things that its subsequent realization will gradually unveil, intuit, attain, I will put together a kite never seen before, multi-colored, beautiful, complex—and capable of flying.

¶ That sordid neighborhood has relocated, the houses have been demolished, new walls erected place of the others—old, and stuck in the ground like milk teeth—the women of that time have died or live on charity, or rot in institutions, some have husbands, children, complain about life. What led me there? My restlessness or the *batuque,* that barely audible beat, endless, that came and went, according to the direction of my walk or the wind, while my hunger waxed and waned, as if fasting had assuaged it? Elephants live in herds and are affectionate; there are, however, solitary, rebellious, intractable individuals. Elephants love each other, and are kind; the solitary ones refuse to participate in incursions and peregrinations, drive the females away, drink alone, bathe alone, grow old alone. I just wanted to be part of a herd, return to some kind of communal life, hold a woman in my arms. In the wide, long and dimly-lit street, crossed by echoes of the *batuque,* dogs were running after me. There were, besides myself, many other men and women, children were begging, an old woman squatting next to a pile of trash moaned a suppliant song. The song was coming from another throat buried in the trash, but the dogs ignored everything, everybody, people and song, they only saw me, barked at my feet, a pack of flashing throats. Go back? I had nowhere to go, returning was the same as going on, as not returning, no voice was waiting for me. A girl in gray was looking at me shyly, leaning against a doorway. People were dancing inside, some of the men wore hats, all with blank faces, straight backs, bowlegged. My hands were cold. The scattered dogs followed the scents of the night, bristling, their ears perked up, blue, black, green, the color of lead. I saw how skinny they were. It was a gay buxom woman with hair à la Robespierre and a shaved nape who took my arm and led me inside. The one in gray—I saw, at a glance, that she was not older than fifteen—looked at me again, and I thought, one of those fleeting thoughts, that not even there did I have any choice in life.

|| Our brother the priest had had a bad night, and we had spent it giving him medicines, tea, massages, preparing hot foot baths. We made a point of not alarming the neighbors, the sick man was our penance and our opportunity to be useful. We were glad, even though afflicted, when he needed us. In the morning he had finally fallen asleep; so had we, exhausted. I was awakened by the noise, the suffocated cries, Helônia's sobs. "It's over!" I ran out barefoot, he was snoring. Then I heard the tapping of the crutch in the living room, Nassi Latif was leaving and my sister was following him in tears, her arms raised. When she saw me barefoot, she screamed that I was spying on

77

her. I slapped her: "I'm not one of your kind." Nassi turned around: "Have you two lost your mind? I'm never coming back here again." "So much the better. The neighbors must be talking. It's not proper for two virgins living alone with their bed-ridden brother to receive a man every day. And on top of that a man whose intentions are unknown." Nassi Latif lifted his crutch and began to laugh, that squeaking laugh. "Who's crazy enough to badmouth you? You've both been off the market for centuries! Next to you Miss Hahn is a baby! Go to hell, you old fools!" After he left, Helônia told me the cause of her despair, Latif had found a job, he was leaving with the circus, to be some kind of guardian or caretaker for Hahn. Helônia's lamentations: "He said we're old. We're no children, I know. But love, at times, comes a little late. I always was a serious girl, accomplished and full of virtues. There was even a time when I knew how to embroider; and my brother swears, even nowadays, that he never knew anyone who could darn socks like me. I did take a fancy to the lieutenant when I was a child. His uniform was a dream. He always ignored me. Everybody has ignored my charms until now. You know I'm not lying: in my whole life Latif was the first young man to show any interest in me." As much as I tried, I could not remember the lieutenant she had taken a fancy to. It must have been a long time ago.

⊖ My grandmother is doing the dishes in the kitchen. Dead air, dead sounds, inert clarity envelop me. The cot creaks. Seeing the town on a Monday did not change anything. I keep thinking about what happened to me yesterday afternoon, even though I know that the experience will not be renewed. The feeling of futility caused by this search heightens the awareness, now sharper, of my poverty in relation to the present. I say to myself: "It's understandable that a man would turn to the past, if there is a fruitful purpose in this search. As for me, I look for the past because I do not have the courage to reshape— or shape—the course of my days." Writing. Would I find salvation in that? The indispensable and difficult apprenticeship scares me. They are taking down the circus, the sun is burning on my head. Observing the elephant, I think about her infallible sense of smell, her sharp hearing, I remember the old man who spoke to me yesterday. Hunters looking for this animal, capable of destroying entire villages in a matter of minutes, use spiderwebs to gauge which way the wind is blowing, in order not to give themselves away. Spiderwebs are instruments of cunning, they help deceive elephants. Silence, perseverance, courage, webs, senses on the alert, these are the weapons I will have to obtain in order to round up the words, then break them with goad and baths. Which tricks will I have to teach them? But writing is a way—not the most effective one—to break out of my exile. I cross the sun-drenched streets like a drunk. A man's fundamental decisions never present themselves by chance, suddenly; as in a work of art, we reach them slowly, by means of enlightenments, and above all maturity, effort, meditation, practice. Many are taking a nap during this hot hour; only a bird insists on singing. In the same moment in which, suddenly, I conceive of the space around me as made of blinding sheets of glass, this difficult decision, surely born in my mind long ago, after a long and secret gestation, manifests itself, and I accept it: I must look for contentment and peace in my life, with energy. A conquest; not a remembrance. But I am still like someone who mentally takes it upon himself to go on a journey, without knowing that he needs to create in his own soul the conditions to overcome his habits, his fears, and leave. My grandmother is putting away the dishes and silverware she has washed.

⊦ Arousing everyone's curiosity, my kite is up in the sky, as original as the one of the pastoral play, while another one, red, draws near. Around me, looking at it condescendingly, are my relatives, whom I called over. Not once do they utter the words of praise that I would like so much to hear. But this is not enough to quell my excitement: I feel that I have triumphed over them, raising up above their indifference this new object, which their minds could never have conceived. My exultation is undone a second later. Seeing that at the end of the red kite's tail, long and convulsive like a wounded snake, someone has maliciously fastened a piece of glass which, with a quick and precise maneuver, has just cut my string, I do not know what to do yet. I am still holding up my arm, even though the tension of the falling kite has left the string dead. I cannot imagine how they knew, these people whose faces I cannot make out, my vision blurred by despair, that I was the owner, or the author, of the kite, the kite which is crashing out of control—and even now, in my eyes, more splendid than ever—over the circus' poles, over the steeples, the square, the crowd and the trees and which, drawing everybody in its direction, relegates Hahn, for a moment, to a secondary position. A nightmarish vision, shattered and anguishing. My own hands, among fifty others, try to grab it in vain. I think it is within my reach—whereas it is unattainable, by some kind of evil spell. Others, rapacious, seize the prey, but only to destroy it, its sticks and colors fall apart in a matter of seconds, explode in every direction as a sob explodes in my mouth, choking me. Then they surround me. They shout, they run around me and—I will never know why—they throw stones at me. In my growing anger, I try to grab one of these demons, hit him, roll over with him. But they flee; and the jeering breaks out again. Impotent, I look near and far, in search of help. A stone hits me somewhere, my rage suddenly leaves me, I need shelter, it does not matter what. I see a tree, the top of the tree, I muster up my strength, run, throw my arms around its trunk.

¶ There was something old-fashioned in the way I made love to that woman. She asked me what city I was from, did not seem to believe me, told me she could not find anyone like me anymore. Does that change too? The way a man goes to bed with a whore? She was very fat, shapeless body, her shoulders and kinky hair drenched in cheap perfume, maybe to mask the smell of the men she had been with before me. She had left the light on; the ceaseless music made the room vibrate. I was staring at her feet, wide, with ankles deformed by a rough life, and toenails painted bright red, asking myself if with the girl in gray I would have entered, for a moment, the community of men, escaped my solitude for a little while, and thinking almost with joy that soon I would be in the street, with the dogs barking around my legs. Oséas was waiting for me. With me at his side he made his way through the dogs which did not even look at me (now I had the smell of that world on me), he took me to a bar three blocks away, bought me some wine, started to talk about women and laughed at the coincidence that had given him a chance to *catch me red-handed.* I heard him indistinctly, barely made him out in the distance, in a white cloud. This was, then, the cloud that separated me from my fellow men. I saw it the way impostors claim to see the evil spirit tormenting us at our side. Resisting the impulse to stretch my hand out toward the mist enveloping Oséas, I thought about Hahn, in her isolation. I was seized by the desire to buy her, take her far away, to join the brothers of her own kind and species, in the Congo or Burma, to offer her the companionship, the love I was not capable of. I grabbed Oséas' hand: "I'm going to get married. A man needs to cry at times. I need to cry, Oséas, today, tonight. But in whose arms? I'm going to get married, it does not matter how, or to whom!" I gulped down the last glass, strode out into the street, starving, not the least bit desperate, drunk bold and happy. Alone again, in the silence of the night, my excitement vanished: I could hardly believe I had experienced it. I crossed my hands behind my back and slowly walked on.

‖ I have known scores of old ages, not to say hundreds. Nobody can teach me what it means to be old. I have seen people age ten years after a trip of a few months, twenty after an operation, thirty after the death of a son. But always by leaps, in the night of absences. With Helônia it was different; I saw her age by the hour, at five in the afternoon looking different from the way she looked at four, stooping more every morning, becoming forgetful, absent, speaking of the events of the previous day as if they had taken place years before. A memorable and bitter week. Those were my brother's last days. I had to face those hours alone, since Helônia, if I asked her to get some medicine, did not come back, looked at the sick man with indifference, went to bed at the most inappropriate hours, wandered around the house at night, speaking to ghosts, to herself, or to images of our past. I prayed to God to keep her on her feet, at least for a month or two, it would be too much for me to take care of two invalids at the same time.

⟋ Having agreed with Bartolomeu to meet at the reservoir, I refrained from taking my nephew along. You can see almost the entire town from here, it is a privileged spot, in this flat region. Formerly there was a hospital in this same place: the Retreat. The people who suffered from smallpox came here in stretchers, they were kept apart from those who were not sick. Later, smallpox became rare; and as this was the highest point in town, the hospital was demolished and the reservoir built; next to it, they put benches, swings among the trees for the children. At eight in the morning on Sundays the gate opens; at six, it closes. An excessive schedule: almost nobody goes up the steep battered red clay path in the afternoon. It is always on sunny mornings, after Mass, that families fill the place and children's voices ring in the clear air like swords clashing. In the afternoon people prefer to go to the movies, walk around the streets, watch the train go by, a kind of god or hieroglyph of our common dreams, symbol of the journey we all long to take. So the two of us are alone, holding hands, next to the invisible waters that supply the town at our feet. The silence all around is like an absolution. We exchanged few words. We walked under the trees, played on the swings, spoke to each other across the reservoir, through the vents, making our voices reflect on the water we could not see, hidden in that huge covered well, where every sound reverberated and, in a manner of speaking, fragmented into rays of light. It was then that he told me, a hundred feet away from me and when we could not see each other, in a frightened voice, for the first time, the only time, that he loved me. After these words, he did not have the courage to look at me. Holding hands, quiet, looking at the roofs between walls and fences, the towers, the greens and grays immersed in a peace which removes us from the earth and its differences, its rigors, we are not aware of time passing or of an impending storm forming in the cloudless sky. Our hands, earlier joined in bliss, tighten their grip with fear.

It is a world of low black clouds, casting a shadow over the earth like an eclipse, a premature nightfall. Neither of us has a watch, it is impossible to know how long it will be till the closing of the gate. The five twenty train from Recife, if it were on time, could be our reference point. But who knows if we have not missed it? If we run downhill, it will take us at least five minutes to pass the gate, cross the street and find shelter. What to do, though, if this rain, which looks like it will be hard, catches us midway? In two minutes, I will be soaked; my summer dress glued to my body, I will not be able to cross town. But if they close the gate, we will be trapped. Startled, we see the train emerge, very far off, its big headlight on. Maybe it is late, as it often happens: aren't the town lights on, in the growing and oppressive darkness? The trees have grown dark too, the ground is taking on a nocturnal color, we look at the afternoon, we look at each other, every time finding the other's anxious face again, and this sight magnifies our uneasiness. Is this voice, so similar to my nephew's, his? "Many people died of smallpox here. They were buried here, not in the cemetery, among these trees." Trying to erase the image of his livid face from my eyes, I exclaim to myself: "This is absurd, absurd!" I do not want to allow his words and fear to cast a spell on me. Despite my efforts, the fear of being trapped, of spending the night here, with the ghosts of the people who died of smallpox, is growing. At the same time, I dare not go down, run down the slope: the clouds seem more and more about to break open, crash down upon us. His mouth on my breasts, slowly sucking them, the two of us sheltered by the covered deck of the reservoir, indifferent to the rain pouring around us. I feel that I have calmed him down, taking him under a mantle, a protection whose existence I myself was not aware of. I did not think. Opening my blouse, I undid my bra, pulled his head toward me, with both hands. I feel that I am giving him, through his mouth, like food, something of my twenty years, and, looking ahead in the future, I intuitively know that I am plunging into a sacred zone forever. I am, at this very hour, a memory forming, being born in the rain.

⌐ Indistinct multitude, sad troop. All of us had known for a week that the elephant would leave today. It has been raining all afternoon, so Hahn is leaving deep footprints in the ground. I cannot see her, as she is way out front; I hear her countless cries of contentment, frightening the Raven perched on the Hydra and alerting the Wolf to the Centaur's raised lance. Luckily the cereal merchant refused to accompany her in the lamented beginning of her voyage; my parents would not let me go out in the streets, unsupervised, after eight. So the two of us go, Adélia and I, mutual guardians, walk hand in hand, happy, before the Virgin's one hundred and ten eyes, under whose influence we act and dream tonight. Fighting against all odds for her love, I tell her my misadventures: the cruelty of the other boys, who destroyed my kite, the persecution, the stoning. My rage, I hide.

—Why did you run to a tree?

—Nobody was on my side. They were all against me.

When I threw my arms around the tree to climb it, I felt the burning. A tree asp.

—On your hand?!

—I wish! Here, on my face.

—Did they put something on it, at home?

—No. They thought it was funny. It hurt like hell.

Adélia kisses me where the asp stung me. The crowd's tramping, their unintelligible voices. Children, grown-ups. We must be very far from town already; even so, we keep following the elephant. Even I, who rarely went to see her, feel suddenly sad about her departure. Why?

—You'll see, when you grow up. Things aren't always as easy as they look. If only I could have a child! Just like you.

—I wouldn't want to be your son.

—No?

—You're so beautiful. I'd like to be your brother. Nephew. Or cousin. Cousin would be best.

I say this and a hard rain starts falling from the starry sky. Hahn, who has found a big puddle of water, sucks it up with her trunk and blows big sprays of mud in the air. Instead of running like the others Adélia and I stand still, serious, looking at each other. Covered with mud, the only immobile beings in the stampede. My chest shows through my shirt, the woman's clothes cling to her body, and our souls, hidden inside us, become exposed too. I enter my friend, I enter a market, she is waiting for me, I take her hand and make my way, make my way with her, naked, into the market, through her body. Canvas tents, prostitutes, horses with pack saddles, merchants, covered wagons, pots of farm honey, crocheted tablecloths, color- ful hammocks, straw mats, clay animals, fruit, vegetables, kites. Adélia bends, picks up a red Indian and walks to- ward me, barefoot, naked, the kite fluttering a little above her hair, like a canopy in a procession, the restless shadow staining the white body. Her dress wet, Adélia penetrates me and discovers in my pupils, crouched, peering out of his hiding place and crying, a precocious man. She smiles understandingly and strokes my damp hair.

¶ A light pole had fallen, or the generator had broken down. There was a black-out in town. Small groups kept coming out of the streets that lead to the square. The circus was dismantled, everything had already been shipped off by train or in the two old trucks. Only Hahn was left, happy, in the moonlight. People leaning out of windows, standing on the courtyard benches, on the steps of the church, on the cornices, on the curbstones, on the roofs. And I, hands behind my back, among the crowd, my eyes fixed on the trunk raised up to the full moon. We wanted to say good-bye to the elephant for the last time. Bicycle lights coiled in the dusty air, lassoing the crowd. Among the shadows I saw Armando's face, his lost ex- pression, his ethereal eyes, his right hand in his coat pocket. He had not come for Hahn; he wanted to see the moonlit courtyard. He likes the moonlight. When the moon is out, he cannot see the garbage dump, the dirty walls, the drunks' faces. A small effort, and he discovers a fjord. Or some of the animals he kept inventing in his oils. There

was something of an ancient ritual in the slowly march-
ing crowd. Someone was singing that *Aida's* March we
knew so well. Other voices, little by little, joined the one
that had started. Where did I read about the case of the
elephant that, for twelve years—yes, twelve—traveled alone
along the Bengal Bay, from island to island, covering hundreds of miles? What was it looking for? And how long
have I been walking in this town, gulf of consternation,
in search of something that may not even exist? Two young
women in front of me were carrying leafy fronds raised
above their heads. I felt a hunger to take their arms, wander off with them, singing like the others. How many
women would go, besides them? Would there not be,
among all of them, one real and fictitious at the same
time, to dispel the invisible cloud that separates me from
life? None? I exclaimed in a hoarse voice: "Good-bye,
Hahn!" She certainly did not know what deep blessing,
what essential hope she was depriving me of. The girls
with the fronds, smiling, looked back. Embarrassed, I
turned down an alley. Adrift once again, screaming inside, I took to the sleeping streets.

|| Standing on the porch, in front of the frail corpse—
my left hand holding the candle, the right pressed against
the wall—I did not know which way to go, what to do.
The body was illuminated by the moon from the waist
down; the tips of its toes brushed the ground. How had it
happened? Sitting next to the priest, in his death throes,
I could hear everything: children blowing their trumpets,
the animal's bellowing, the little circus orchestra playing

the music heard so many times, the voices, then the levy of recruits singing. I asked Helônia to go to the neighbors, call someone. She did not pay attention to me: in a chair, facing the closed window, she did not move. It was I who went around knocking on the neighbors' doors, trying to get people to help me with the prayers. It seemed that nobody was home, everybody wanted to see the elephant. After that, I must have fallen into a daze. I put the candle into our brother's hands, alone, calling Helônia in vain. After he was dead, I called out for her aloud, hunting her down through the darkness of the house with the funeral candle. The people's singing, already very far away, followed in the wake of Hahn; so did Nassi Latif, once more without a destination, led by his folly, his restlessness. That madman. And Helônia, where was she hiding, with her consuming passion? I went back to the bedroom, near the deceased. Was there a moan, a creak, a presentiment then? I will never know. All I know is that I went out, and found my sister suspended above her empty slippers, by a silk rope, brushing the ground with her toes. Like those earthbound birds that get off the ground but cannot fly. Poor, poor Helônia, so full of hopes, with so much of her life still to be lived.

⚞ "I am writing to you by candlelight, with tears in my eyes. My father was transferred: we are leaving town. Meanwhile, yesterday, coming back from the reservoir, I was thinking about what I could do to avoid seeing you again. Not that I am ashamed of what happened. It was so beautiful! But we must resign ourselves: I am a woman, you are a boy, and ours is an impossible love. Besides, these last days, without telling you anything, I have thought of joining the circus, working in the dramas, as an actress. I have read Eleonora Duse's life. It must be such a wonderful thing to feel in your body, in your face and voice the ability to make others believe that you are someone else! Forgive me for not having told you about this. But it is because I knew: soon we would be apart. In the light of what happened yesterday, I think the time has come. I therefore ask you, by what is most sacred to you: *do not try to speak to me*. Let us keep intact in our memory yesterday's picture, the final scene, the two of us in the rain, suspended over the town. Like two angels.

I am beginning to hear, without any anguish, Hahn's musical piece, sung in chorus. I heard that a lot of people are going to see her off at the edge of town. How can anybody understand such a gesture, when several among that crowd persecuted us mercilessly, so many times, with the same song they are now singing so innocently? Could it be because there's no tenderness in their lives? Yes, maybe it was our love that irritated them and that they were trying to cloud (we were vulnerable, unfortunately) with their mockery. And if they all follow the elephant, *it is because they love her*, and they have nothing better. Even I, is it not possible that I, before I saw you, loved her too? But this love, my darling, this love of theirs, is as unreasonable as mine for you and yours for me. Let us part, then, and forever. Good-bye. Things without a future spoil before long. They are destined to end soon.

I remember when Hahn, illuminated by your eyes, looked blue to me in the afternoon sky. Now she is leaving, I will never see her again. I, too, take leave from our misunderstood love, which had such a short life and made me so happy. Despite everything, it was the most beautiful thing I have known in my entire life. I will always love you. Your. . .Hahn."

⊖ From the bus—the last one to Recife—I can hardly recognize the moonlit town. Matters I need to solve are on my mind. The present is a not entirely healthy tissue, in which dead areas continue to exist, affecting the living parts. How to remove them? How many things in me can I save from disintegration? I hear the sound of steps, think that cattle are blocking the street, see the crowd. They are all silently following the elephant, the procession is like one accompanying a funeral. A small band follows at her side, their instruments lowered. "She's a dead animal—I say angrily. She's going to the cemetery on her own feet. She dies in every town she goes to." I see myself following the trail of dead things, like everyone else in the crowd. As if answering me, one of the players, in a cutaway coat and bowler hat, puts an oliphant to his lips and emits a prolonged sound, in the direction of the stars. A confused roar—there are hundreds, perhaps a thousand people—comes from the crowd. The band starts the first phrases of *Aida*'s Triumphal March in a slightly adulterated version. As if by contagion, the music is repeated, the bus driver tries to accompany it with the horn, and the man with the oliphant goes on indifferent to the melody and the rhythm, blowing like a madman. Hahn, rugs on her forehead and on her back, seems to liven up, taking on infinite meanings in my eyes. I cannot stop looking at that huge and fantastic moonlit beast until the man with the oliphant approaches. I stare at him as if he—and not I—were shouting these orders: "Bury the dead. Write, no matter how or what. Turn the past, a master that today drains and fetters your strength and life, a power conquered by the blood of your days, into a slave, no longer a sovereign entity or a parasite. Let your memories, no longer denied, be the arena where you will exert your choice, which will perhaps fall back on your own deaths, on elephants you will never see again, in order to give everything to the living and thus give life to what has been devoured by Time. Go through the world and its joys, seek love, whet with artfulness your hunger to create." Mangled and uneven, Verdi's music grows louder. Will I be able to obey the shouts of the oliphant? Hahn is moving faster, flapping her ears. She seems winged to me, a translucent animal, almost immaterial, taller than the houses, no longer something dead, but an emblem of everything that is great and impossible, of everything that is greater than us and that, even though we follow for some time, we rarely pursue forever.

The Confused

⌐I'M TIRED. It's almost midnight.

—I'm still on vacation, I can get up late.

⌐But I can't. Oh well, who cares. I can handle one night without sleep. It won't be the first time.

—Are you alluding to me?

⌐Maybe.

—I haven't criticized you, haven't asked any questions, haven't said anything. We haven't spoken since dinner.

⌐There must be something I was condemned to hear today. I can feel it in the air, in my hands. I hope the horror will at least start before daybreak. Tomorrow is Tuesday and I have to work.

One of us got up, or will get up to open the curtains, look at the night. The ceaseless noise of the cars will rise— rose?— from the avenue, whirling around the living room, above the watercolors in their delicate frames, above the leather armchairs with red cushions, around the lit lamp. The stars twinkling, looking shaken by the noise of the city that never sleeps. We are holding hands, whose is burning? We are staring at the bare wall.

—Today I had another relapse. I promised I'd never do it again. But I can't keep my word, I simply can't. It was just as bad as ever, I'm all shaken up.

└Then there's nothing you can do about it.

—There must be something.

└How long am I going to have to live in this hell? Will I have to wait until the end of my life?

—You need to be more understanding.

└Words again. Useless as always.

—They're not useless.

└I'm sick of this. We went three weeks without this odious thing. Perfect days.

—We were together morning, afternoon and night. I couldn't doubt…myself.

—I only had to leave for a few hours for it to start all over again. Am I just staring into the eyes of a blind man, then?

—Let me explain.

└I'd rather not hear it.

—I must hear it.

└And on top of everything else, this too: a total lack of compassion. I can accept your not trusting me, even though there's no reason. But why tell me? It's cruel.

—I want to be honest.

└I despise this kind of honesty to the point of nausea. It makes me sick. What honesty are you talking about? I surrender. I trust. I yield to the embraces, the kisses. And what's behind the caresses? My eyes are closed. My lips meet my lips. And two eyes are scrutinizing me. Is this being honest?

—When we love each other all my doubts disappear.

—How am I to know? How am I going to believe you?

—I'm telling you. All my doubts disappear. When we're together there's something that gives me faith again. I think that it's going to be like this forever, that all misunderstandings are over and that there won't be any problems between us again. All of a sudden, I find myself alone. And I start all over again.

⌐I Why not be suspicious when I'm here? I could be here, by myself, naked and thinking about another man. Secretly comparing the way he embraces me. The way he....

—Stop it! If I destroy this, this certainty, the last and only one, what do I have left?

⌐I I don't care. Not even that exists for me. I'm also beginning to doubt myself, I no longer know myself, I don't know who I am anymore.

Which of us opens the gilt cigarette case nervously, snaps the lighter shut decisively after staring at the flame for a long time? One gets up, walks, the other remains seated, then gets up, we cross the living-room, one sits down again, we remain standing, back to back, together.

—When I saw that I was alone, I went to bed. I started to think how close we had become during these three weeks, and how all misunderstandings had ceased. We didn't have just a few happy and quiet moments. All those days were filled with happiness and peace. I saw myself at the beach again, my serenity in the water, my body, my thighs, I remembered how hot our skin would get in the afternoon…I regretted my old doubts and thought that after eight years we had conquered what we'd been looking for all this time. Then I went to the bathroom and I saw: everything was dry.

⌐I did take a shower. Maybe it was because of the heat.

—Yes.

⌐And I dried the tub with a cloth.

—I've never done that.

⌐I always do.

—First I say that it was the heat. Then, that the tub is dry because I wiped it with a cloth. Why these two versions? These lies are what kills me.

⌐I'm not lying.

—Yes I am!

⌐One thing doesn't necessarily exclude the other. This is absurd.

—The towel was dry too. I said to myself that it didn't matter. But at this point I had already started to remember the recommendations I had made to myself. Not to go out, take advantage of the last afternoons of vacation, stay home and work on the article on Lawrence's correspondence.

⌐It was a mistake. It's impossible not to make mistakes with certain people. One always makes mistakes.

—There are parts of us that should never be divulged.

But I have to be absolutely honest. Like Lawrence. He
was honest.

⌐–I'm not Lawrence.

—What I felt, what I feel, is like what happened to me
when I was alone as a kid and was alone. What turned me
on? Pictures of women? Pornography ? Solitude did. Im-
perceptibly, irresistibly, I sought pleasure in myself, an
anxious and immature pleasure. Only to sink into de-
pression afterwards; and start everything all over again as
soon as I was alone in my room or in the bathroom again.
Solitude, for me, was the same as a naked woman. Now
it's like the presence of a rival.

⌐–There is no rival.

—That's what I think when we're together. There is no
one else, there never was, we both love each other. But
when I'm alone!

⌐–I take pleasure in arousing pity.

—I deserve pity.

I went to the bedroom, I stay in the living room, I
slowly put on my *négligé*, I feel my face, my beard is starting to grow out, I return to myself, my steps are light, I
remain seated, I did not get up.

⌐–It's best to get it over with. I'm tired.

—I thought that insisting on my spending the afternoon at home was a ruse.

⌐–I didn't insist.

—A ruse to keep me from going out or talking on the
phone. Why didn't I take a shower if there was time? I
wanted to gain a few minutes, or half an hour, arrive a

little earlier at some encounter agreed upon two weeks ago, or maybe arranged at the hotel, during a moment of absence, maybe at the hairdresser's, or at the manicure, how do I know? I must say that I didn't use the phone.

⌐I don't believe it. There was a phone call at one point. When I answered they hung up.

—Who do I think it was?

⌐I have no idea.

—Who was it?

⌐I don't know. Honestly, I don't know.

—I didn't call. But I went through all your purses, one by one. I said to myself: you're doing something foolish, you could come across some paper you aren't responsible for, but which would incriminate and destroy you, and that would be useless after all, since I don't have the courage to leave.

—Did I find anything?

—This: the name of a man. This address. I want to know who he is.

—I don't remember.

—I turned pale.

—Who wouldn't? I'm furious!

—Why, if it's me who's been insulted?

—I'm the one who's been insulted.

—Who is he?

—I don't know. Maybe a shoemaker. Maybe he's a hairdresser, recommended by the girls at the office. The handwriting is mine. But I don't remember writing down that address. Or maybe a man I will love and who'll offer me a little peace at last. Who won't torture me and won't torture himself every day of his life. With this hunger for possession, for property. With these ties, these traps, these knives of suspicion. I wish I were dead!

—Who's the man?

—For God's sake! There isn't any man, no other man, no man. None.

—And this name? I need to know.

—From time to time everybody finds among their papers notes they no longer know why they took.

—You can remember if you really want to.

—When a madman becomes irrevocably insane, when he can't escape madness and behave like normal people, everybody else gives in and acts as if they were crazy too. Not deliberately. They do it without realizing and because there's no other solution. This is the problem when you live with lunatics. So here's the result: I'm making the effort I demand of myself, I'm trying to remember. I need to get out of this. I need to get out of this once and for all.

—Why don't I, then?

I get up, my eyelids heavy with sleep, go to the bathroom, hold my finger on the chrome button for a long time, listening to the violent flush of water, taking pleasure in it, then I go back to bed. I walk around the bed placed in the middle of the room. I walk around and around it, and this walking around is like slowly drinking an inebriating wine.

—I'm thinking of when I had my kidney operation.

Why do they always hurt whenever there are scenes like this? They grafted some tissue from my intestines onto my kidneys. And then they waited. They had done what they could. The rest wasn't up to them, they couldn't make the tissue adapt to its new function.

—What am I trying to get at?

└I don't know. I wonder what this memory might mean. My body responded, didn't let the graft die. I survived. What for? I wish I knew.

—We've had, I and I, many good times.

└To hell with them! I don't want any good times. I want trust and a little respect. Those good times are full of poison.

—Everything in life has its negative side.

└Here all sides are negative, even the ones that look positive. This is hell.

Someone pulls the curtains apart, slides the window open, everything stays the same, this is hell, the petrified air coats this open window with bitumen, this is hell.

└It's hell. I think people at times are thrown in hell during their lifetime without knowing it. They keep going around in circles, passing over the same points for eternity. I want to get out of this, it wasn't to suffer like this that my body overcame death. But how, if I've lost my identity and I don't know who I am anymore? We're like two bodies buried together, gnawed by the earth, their bones mixed together. I don't know who I am anymore.

—It's because we love each other. We've become confused, each of us is himself and also the other.

╰─This isn't love. You don't lose your identity in love, but in the office, in collective life; or when solitude is too great, for lack of points of reference. In love, on the contrary, we should find our lost identity again.

—I insist: in love, each is oneself and the other.

╰─All right. What else did I find, today, in my search for *oneself and the other*?

—I'd rather not say anything. That's over.

╰─Now I'm already poisoned, I've conformed to madness. I want to know.

I walk around the bed on which I lie, we are panting, not with passion, but with fatigue. I would like to ignore these footsteps fencing me in, tying me up in knots of affliction, terror and distress, I would like to sit, or lie down, I would like to be what I want to be, I am exhausted, I do not even have the strength to speak, to ask for the footsteps to cease.

—I lifted the mattress, to see if I could find any other paper, I rummaged through the wastebasket. I tried to write. It was impossible, the temptation to keep searching wouldn't leave me. I put Lawrence and his letters aside, started to leaf through our books. At random, and then systematically. Clammy hands. I said to myself that I was being unfair, but I didn't stop, I kept searching, it was as if I needed to find something. It was like a fit, a seizure.

╰─Did I find anything?

—Dried rose petals. Did they come from a rose I gave you?

⌐Of course.

─I didn't know. I looked at them, as if roses given by someone else could have a different texture. There was a card, without the name of the addressee. Like many others I received during these years, especially in the beginning. But maybe that one wasn't directed to me. Why was it there?

⌐How do I know? This search is so futile! To know the truth about someone you would have to get into his head, and that's impossible. These searches, this persecution, these anxieties...

─I want to love in a simple, definitive, trusting way.

This silence and the space between us. The voice cutting through the space and the silence, with difficulty, slow, uttering a disturbing hypothesis. (Love, perhaps, is a kind of graft. Not to the kidneys. Somewhere else, maybe in the soul, a graft whose success does not depend on us. No matter how much we want to save it, it can become infected and contaminate us.) Silence again, thick, shock-absorbing, straw and wood shavings between chinaware.

─Am I poisoned then? Are we poisoned?

⌐Not me. Me. Yes, maybe I am too. How can I know, if I don't know who I am anymore?

─It's after midnight.

⌐Way after. It's going to be morning soon. Another circle. The sun is round, round is the earth. Around the earth we make one revolution; and the earth makes another around the sun. And we turn, turn, and always come back to the same point.

Retable of Saint Joana Carolina

First Mystery

Shooting stars and fixed stars, bolids, comets moving across space like reptiles, great nebulas, rivers of fire and magnitude, the orderly agglomerations, space doubled, its amplitudes reflected in the mirrors of Time, the Sun and the planets, our Moon and its four phases, everything weighed on the invisible scale, with pollen in one dish, the constellations in the other, regulating, with the same exactitude, the distance, the vertigo, the weight and the numbers.

⊕ I was with Joana Carolina and her family for many years. There I am, the black girl weighing her (she is so light!) in my hands, beneath Totônia's wide eyes, who asks me: "Is it a normal human being or is it a man?" Because her husband, whose exact name is not known, and who does not have a definite face, sometimes bearded, others shaven, with long hair, or short— even his eyes changed color—only comes home to make babies or other surprises, until he vanishes again on the wings of some journey. Those four children look-

ing at us, lined up on the other side of the bed, holding their obscure destinies in the fists clenched on their
chests, are the traces of those passages without warning, without duration: Suzana, João, Filomena and
Lucina, all picked by me from Totônia's prodigal womb,
from which children drop easily, like ripe fruit. They
say that children are things we plant, promises of sus-
tenance. With all these, Totônia will still end her days
in poverty: Suzana, married to a brute younger than
her, will grow old consumed by jealousy, thinking that
every woman, even her mother, lusts after her husband, an animal, capable of jumping into the bushes,
howling, with priests and statues of saints, with anything reminiscent of women or women's clothes, even
the Devil, with horns, tail, hooves and all, if he appeared to him in a skirt; João, the kind of man who
will not swallow an insult, will live without any security, forever changing jobs and cities, his legs, arms
and fingers bearing the scars of stabwounds and gun-
shots; Filomena, the wife of a gambler, will cultivate all
forms of avarice, incapable of offering even a glass of
water to anyone; Lucina will come in conflict with
Totônia and will deny her hand and word. Only Joana,
Joana Carolina, will give her support, despite her own
poverty: the old woman will die in her care, in her
house, thirty-six years from now, on the Serra Grande
plantation. Lucina will walk three leagues to kneel at
the foot of her bed and ask for her forgiveness, crying.
Neither she, nor Filomena, nor Suzana will offer their

sister any help. In order to get mourning clothes for her children, Joana Carolina, already a widow by then, will buy black fabric on credit. It will be hard to pay this bill. The shopkeeper, as if in charge of the scale that weighs our virtues and sins, will write her a letter, reminding her that we do not know the time of our death and therefore we must be quick about paying off our debts, not to burn in the flames of hell. I will sell a pig, lend the money to Joana Carolina, she will pay the shopkeeper. My words: "Even if you can't give me back what I loaned you, Joana, you won't suffer for it. You're a loyal woman. In your heart, you'll never owe anyone a cent."

SECOND MYSTERY

The house. With the tree and the sun, the first and most common picture drawn by children. It is where the table, the bed and the stove are. The external walls and the roof protect us and keep us from dissolving in the vastness of the Earth; and the inside walls, while allowing isolation, establish rituals, defined relationships between place and activity, reserving the dining room for meals and thus preventing us from begetting our offspring on the tablecloth. Through the doors, we have access to and return from the rest of the universe; from the windows we contemplate it. A band of men makes up a horde, an army, a camp or an expedi-

tion, always something nostalgic and errant; a group
of houses makes up a town, a landmark, a fixed point,
a here, from which paths depart and upon which ambitions and roads converge, which remains stationary
or grows according to its strength, and perhaps will be
destroyed, buried, but even so still shine from under
the ground, in silence, from the darkness, by way of its
name.

☐ It is November, when the directorship of the
Brotherhood of Souls used to change—and perhaps
still does. Joana, who turned eleven the month before,
looks at me with her palms up, unable to explain why
she acted the way she did, intimidated by our green
surplices. In the background, some crosses and a eu-
calyptus. On the left of the group, holding her son's
hand, Dona Totônia, half humble, half angry, is raising
her foot over the scorpions I found among the coins. A
little to the right, with its door open, the Coffer of the
Souls, a small construction like many others scattered
through the town to receive alms from the passers-by,
which has become almost a sanctuary, since some
people light candles or pray for their dead here; and
which I, as Second Treasurer, with a small coffer, many
keys in my hand and a parasol because of the heat,
visited for the first time this Friday. On the ground, as
big as crawfish and still smaller than the copper coins,
the same scorpions that will be crushed by Dona
Totônia, one of which is crawling up our President's

bare arm. Joana's explanation: "I wanted to give something." "But why scorpions? And not, for example, pieces of glass?" "I didn't have any pieces of glass." "What did you do to keep them from raising their stinger?" "They don't bite." Many years from now, Joana will pass by this same place, at night, holding the small hand of Laura, her daughter, who will be trembling with fear, fascinated, seeing the will-o'-the-wisp in the cemetery, this terror mingled with a joy that will permeate her memory, because of the smell of coffee, of toasted bread, coming from the houses of the hamlet, in the afternoon, like a festive noise. The smell of coffee, of bread, is not very common in Totônia's house. Joana does not have many distractions. Not too many weeks ago, she discovered two things that do not cost any money and give her pleasure: going to children's funerals; and a nest of scorpions in the back of the yard. She puts them in a tin can, plays with them; she goes to the cemetery and waits next to the Coffer of the Souls until the smell of coffee and bread blends with the light of the sunset. Here we are, surrounding her, interrogating her, because she decided to put together her two pleasures: she brought the can of scorpions to the funeral, gave the insects as alms for the souls, dropping them through the slit, as if they were money. The President of the Brotherhood cries that nobody can touch a scorpion. Joana Carolina: "I can." She holds them in her closed hands, gently. She lets them go. "If the child can do this, with the help of God I will too."

The President with his sleeve rolled up, his soft white arm. The scorpion going up his wrist, stinger up, doubled, the color of fire; then advancing towards Dona Totônia with the other three that were on the ground; she stamping them out. She grabs her daughter by the arm and leaves. We stay and argue among ourselves, convinced of dealings with the Devil, since we accept him much more easily than angels.

THIRD MYSTERY

The square, the temple. Meeting place. The men gathered for discussion, for leisure, for prayer. Questions and questions, answers, conversations with God, rallies, sermons, speeches, processions, bands, circuses, amusement parks, litters bearing saints' images, poles and flags, merry-go-rounds, stalls, bells pealing, girandoles and fireworks thrown high up in the sky, expanding, in the direction of the towers, the horizontal space of the square.

♂ Joana, barefoot, dressed in white, the breeze blowing in her golden hair, carries the framed image of Saint Sebastian on her breast. Over her shoulders, covering her arms, her hands, and so long that it almost touches the ground, they threw a crocheted tablecloth, with a pattern of centaurs. The thick arrows in the saint's chest seem to pass through it, to be firmly stuck in

Joana. Behind her, in a serpentine line, singing and holding candles in their hands, many women. The December night has not quite fallen yet, there is still some daylight in the air. I can see that Joana's eyes are big and blue; and that her face, even though disfigured, since she is still convalescing, is different from all the others I have seen, firm and delicate at the same time. Crystal dagger. Even I, who have not been in town long, heard about her illness. Half-blind, detached from reality, feverish, her legs paralyzed. Her mother made a vow, if she were healed: a procession with candles, through the streets. So, during the brief span of this glance, the first we exchange, which already joins us, with all that this involves, I simply see in Joana the adolescent snatched from immobility and blindness thanks to a miracle, to come to this encounter with her white feet to discover me. I have, ignorant me, the feeling of having been granted a grace, certain that in this girl triply illuminated—by the afternoon sun, by the candles, by my ecstasy—and in whom the illness, more than a tribulation, was a design to keep her until I emerged, from the entrails of time, this minute, resides the happiness of life, and that by joining myself to her I take possession of a greatness I cannot even imagine and will never understand. The depths of my soul harpooned by her gaze, I offer myself with the utmost candor, imagining that this enthusiasm suddenly born in my spirit can buy peace and joy. I do not know that this arrow shot at the sound of the hymn sung by the women is a seed whose fruits nobody can predict, and that the joys will be almost none in comparison to the pain, the ravages in our lives, especially in Joana's, my victim.

Fourth Mystery

Greenness of the foliage, sun of the arteries, earth's invisible cloak. Instigator of fires, voice of windmills, oar of vessels occasionally broken by lulls in the wind, trail without beginning or bounds of all flying creatures—bats, butterflies, birds of small or great wingspan. Stirrer of oceans, wrath of the whirlwinds, of the hurricanes, of the gales, of the tornadoes. Shepherd of mastodons, of dinosaurs, of gigantic reindeer, herded on blue pastures, whose bones, whose hide and horns turn into rain, into a rainbow.

✓ Our father liked animals. He taught a blackthroated cardinal to ride a goat named Gedáblia, and to spur it on with short whistles. Nô and I will inherit this passion and, in a certain way, it is because of this that, years from now, while our mother, after his death, suffers at the Serra Grande plantation, we will go off into the world, in search of work, leaving her with Teófanes and Laura, our younger siblings still to be born. Then we will take her from the plantation and bring her back to town. Right now we are two kids, lying on banana leaves, our mother bent over us, stirring up the fire with lavender. A nauseating smell fills the entire house, the smell of our ulcerated bodies. Maria do Carmo, our only sister, died two days ago, on the tenth day of the year. It was hot, this January heat that suffocates us all, she was asking for water. She died thirsty. Our father is trying to entertain us with the bird and Gedáblia, but we are not paying attention to him. A train conductor, he is always away from home. When he is off duty he takes us to the woods, catches birds, tries to domesticate them. He earns very little. To help him out, our mother set up a little hotel near the station where other railroad employees could eat. But who wants to sit at a hotel table with this epidemic, smallpox that kills and scars the skin of those who survive? Even if there were clients, our mother would not open the hotel. She has not slept for a week, keeping vigil at our bedstead night and day without knowing where to turn for help. Almost all the doors are bolted, we hardly hear any steps or street vendors' cries, no laughter. We are plunged into a silence punctuated with cries and my dreams are full of menacing ghosts stepping over me and big birds with red heads that fly above me and tear pieces of flesh from my body. But not even this made me hate birds and goats. The owner of Serra Grande will be jealous of his orange grove. In the sadness of those future days, when food will be even scarcer than today, when already there is not much, our source of joy, mine and Nô's, will be the same as our father's: catching young birds, raising them at home, training them. Our revenge on life, an animal that cannot be domesticated. The plantation owner will catch us in his orchard and he will mistake the fledglings in our hands for oranges. Furious, he will complain to our mother. Then she will send us away, we will look for work and one day we will come to get her, proud of ourselves. Smallpox, for Nô, is worse than for me. It will leave his arm, the left one, twisted for a long time. Every day our mother will massage it with sheep fat, until he will be able to move it again, steal young birds with me, and then work, until we will take our mother away and bring her a little of the peace and security that our father, without ever succeeding, wanted to give her.

FIFTH MYSTERY

The slow rotation of water, through its various states. Its oscillation between the tranquillity of cups and floods. Maybe it is a mineral; or a plant, a ship's rigging entangling continents, islands. It may be an animal, a huge fish that has swallowed darkness and abysses, with all of their shells, anemones, dolphins, whales and shipwrecked treasures. It would like to have, perhaps, the definition of stones; yet it never defines itself. Invisible. Visible. Penetrable. Hard. Inimical. Friendly. There exist cyclones, water spouts. Fin strokes? And also the clouds, fruit that, when ripe, rain down. The fish absorbs them and grows. Then this fish, ramate and green, silver and saline, feeds on itself? Drinks its own thirst? Eats its hunger? Swims in itself? We will never know about this elusive, lustral, obscure, clear and vanquishing entity. I have it in my eyes, inside my pupils. Therefore I do not know whether I see it; or if it is seeing itself.

⊙ I saw in that boy, when he came to ask me for Joana's hand, the mark of death. The warning. The sign. I tried to dissuade him. We were people of no means and scarce letters. "It doesn't matter. Since I saw your daughter, in the procession…Forgive me, but I've been thinking of her as my wife since then. I want to protect her so much!" "You're mistaken, she's the one who'll protect you," "I work. I work for the railroad. I will work my way up." "What's your name?" "Jerônimo José." "Senhor Jerônimo, excuse me for telling you this: I've seen few men as frail as you are. I don't mean physically. It's inside. Born to be a goldsmith. Or a miniaturist, wrapped up in your own world, painting Our Ladies, Baby Jesuses. Do you like to read?" "I read a lot." He had no father, or mother. He burst into tears, squeezing my hand, as if I had discovered the weaknesses he tried to hide most. I was always a tough woman. I have two towers on my head, I am the wife, the Church, the earthly one, she who pollutes herself, who delivers children and turns her blood into milk, the frail one. Isn't that what the liturgy says? Well then, if I am weak, I must become as hard as stone. I

am as hard as stone; but I, too, cried. "Joana will marry
you, son. (That is what I called him.) Don't be ashamed
of your childish qualities. Your weakness, your ignorance of things. The visions that the others, almost all
of them, think the ravings of a madman. Those are
merits too." I was not moved by the other requests:
they were vulgar men. But the soul, the presence of a
soul will always stir me. The comings and goings of
that poor boy to set up his house! Four chairs brought
from Natã; a chandelier bought in Recife; a urinal received as a present; two trinkets won at a game of for-
feits; the tie pin sold for the final expenses. Everything
in order to live those ten years, until all of a sudden he
died, with eight thousand reis in his pocket and a few
pennies more scattered among his drawers. He should
have been buried in a blue coffin, like a child. He was
so good that many times I wondered whether Joana
felt pleasure, the pleasure a woman feels, when she lay
with him, so different from the man I had married,
who seemed to have been born just to learn nocturnal
arts, or ripen his flesh with plunges in the river, nights
outdoors, so that I always yielded to his orders, I opened
like the Red Sea before Moses—knowing that in nine
months I would have yet another child with a mouth
and stomach, and not a penny richer—and he crossed
me with his armies of fire and joy, the brightest flags
unfurling on the poles. This may be the reason why
the lives of my other daughters were so dismal, Suzana
poisoned with lust, Filomena's nose and nails crooked

with avarice, Lucina angry at everybody, even me. João Sebastião, a vagabond without any direction in his life, must be his father's doing, his reflection. But why, Totônia, do you attribute such vague origins to your children's faults? Why should such serious mistakes be born of a tendency of the flesh, over which, all things considered, nobody has any control, and not as a result of your usual behavior, of your lack of authority? Even if you are wrong, if you are hard on yourself, you must admit that the mistakes of your children are the children of your mistakes, but without letting this distress you, because to believe ourselves capable of mistakes is a sign of humility, Totônia—and it is prideful to think that mistakes and errors are always for the others. Even if you lost your bearings and your judgment in the upbringing of your children, isn't this Joana the reward? Think of her serenity. She could throw up her arms, blame it on herself, blame it on the circumstances, wish to do again what can be done only once, she could be afraid, or faint. She does not make a banner of her pain, she keeps it like a secret. In the recesses of her soul. She does not want to block out the sun that comes in through the window; or silence the drums, the basses, the guitars, the flutes and the maracas filling the streets, this Carnival Sunday; nor does she think that it would be better to die on another day. She knows that no days are better than others for adversities; that men can see the sun, but the sun cannot see men; and that people, when they are happy, have a right to their joy, because everybody has his days of tears, and one man's sorrow is not always everybody else's. And who better than Joana could forget, get these truths off her mind, for today? She could tell me that if she had gone to Belém do Pará when her husband called her he would still be alive. Strange! That boy, so delicate, had great rages, unexpected gestures, as if he concealed within himself a determined wing, ready to fly for him when necessary. The Englishmen from the railroad wanted and demanded that he close the hotel, a subsidy unworthy of a second class conductor. Worthy, for the gringos, meant to receive the pay of a beggar and starve. "Either you close the hotel, or you're fired." He lost his job, bought two cans of kerosene, poured them over two cars of the line, set them on fire, left for Belém, took up the practice of law, got a job as judge in the interior, wrote to Joana, asking her to join him. She asked me if I would go. "How? Old as I am, almost seventy? At this age, the only trip I have left is to the cemetery, if God grants me the grace of not dying consumed by flames or drowned in one of those floods that take even cattle and rooftops with them. But you must go." She would not. Of my children, she was the only one left, the others were of no help to me. She came to see me, went to church with me, invited me to her house on Sundays, she even gave me presents: a bowl, one or two dozen pins, a canary trained by Jerônimo. She was my support. My strength. My source of joy. The opposite of solitude. He understood, did not complain and came back. Joana apologized. His reply: "It was my mistake to call you. It was a good opportunity, I was tempted. Many people may think you should have come. But home is not always where the husband is; it's where peace of mind is." He showed me his new law books and a little box with stamps. Great Western sued him for arson, he defended himself, won the suit. He had courage, but not to throw to the winds; just enough to get along. So, when they explained to him, in the Barra Plantation, the feelings that existed between the Barnabós and the Câmara family, who had called him to represent them in a dispute over some land, he decided to come back immediately. "Any lawyer who takes the job will get a bullet in his head. Besides, you know: the Câmaras aren't any saints either. Is anyone right in a dispute between devils? Everybody there is an outlaw. I'll tell you something else, if I were you I wouldn't be slow about it. I'd turn my horse around and go home. Those people are too fond of ambushes." When he got on his horse he felt the pain in his chest and realized he was going to die. Death, too, likes to do away with its victims in an ambush. His horse is evidence of what the trip was like for this son-in-law of mine. "Joana, I came to die at home." The horse's hooves shattered like glass. Jerônimo lay down in the hammock, asked for some tea, called his five children. The water was boiling, Joana brought the drink, so hot it must have burnt the dying man's lips. He did not even manage to finish it all. Isn't this enough for Joana to despair? Instead, she cuts the bread for her five children's meal, two on her left, the

others on her right. Through the window, masquerad-
ers look at the dead man in the coffin, one of them has
a banjo on his chest; the horse is resting, a bundle of
veins, with purple eyes and legs covered with blood;
two visitors on each side, two angels, two candlesticks,
one of my arms is hanging at my side, the other
stretched out, my hand on Jerônimo's forehead; above
us hovers one of the birds he domesticated, which,
after flying away, will come back through the window
in the afternoon and quietly light on Joana's slippers.

Sixth Mystery

—What does a man do, when he's in need?

—He strikes out and stabs. He kills jaguars in the
water, hawks in the woods, whales in the air.

—What does he invent and use, in such impossible
circumstances?

—Eye and cunning, arm and string, horns and horses,
falcon, silence, steel, caution, hounds and explosion.

—Doesn't he have any compassion?

—No. He has majesty.

—In his powerlessness?

—It's his condition.

—Does he always find his prey? His catch? With his
dark net, his luminous arrow, his fishhook of fire, his
hard harquebus, can he always discover the animal in
the air, in the shadows, at the bottom of the abyss?

—Not all the time. And in the end he is executed.

—By what greater executioner?

—Death, who devours fish and fishermen, hunted and hunters with his cold tooth.

♈ I look much more like the Devil than a man here. *Vade retro.* That is not what women thought of me. A fishing pole over my shoulder, a string of fish in my hand, I look at Joana with the eye of one searching the bottom of a river. Goatee, the brim of my hat turned up on both sides of my head, like horns. Terrifying, an evil creature. I was not like that. I bathed in the well, with soap, my hat was immaculate, its brim low over my eyes, I had sideburns, liked hunting, not fishing. I approached women meekly, I had a weakness for widows and married women, I never took advantage of innocent girls; virgins were safe with me, and no son of mine was ever denied protection. That is why I went broke, squandered everything my father had put together; and of the twenty-two children I gave my name to, by eighteen different women, none, after they grew up, recognized me as his father. I am sure they saw me as I never was: the beard of a goat, hooves, smell of sulfur. Joana, the teacher, wards me off with the ruler and the ferule in her hand, forming with the two instruments a kind of open compass; with the other arm she protects her five children. Nô, the live wire; Álvaro, the smart one; Teófanes, the resigned; Laura, the pensive; Maria do Carmo, the second by that name, who will also die as a child. The foolishness of my father, of an old man, to bring a teacher to our lands. To teach these wretches? Anyway, since the town paid for it, and we only had to provide the teacher with a house…She traveled six leagues each month, three one way and three back, to get her salary. There are so many miserable people in this world! To leave her house, with a string of children, to teach from seven to two in the afternoon, without eating even a crust of bread, getting letters and numbers into the heads of thirty mules. Only to receive, in the end, written on the blackboard by one of them, her pay, her reward: "The teacher is a bitch." She arrived around Holy Week. Her age, I do not know exactly. She was in her March, approaching the end of her summer. She spent over seven years here in Serra Grande. When she left, she had aged twenty: her face, hardened, sunburnt, had lost its bloom; her golden hair bleached out, her back bent—and she had lost some teeth. Even so, at times I felt uneasy when I looked at her. A serenity came from within her, like the one we see in the images of saints, the coarsest ones. A sound of eternity. My conscience is clear: I did everything humanly possible to go to bed with her. It was not easy, it took over a year for the first assault. She had a fortification I had to penetrate little by little, an invisible protection, of composure and silence, a dome of strength, nobility. She looked me straight in the eye, with her blue eyes, stern as a master's. I set her up comfortably, in the best house, near the old slave quarters. Wide door, front window, another on the side, a large room for her useless classes; the hallway served as a kitchen. The rooms left much to be desired; dark as caves, you had to descend a few steps to get to them; but they were good enough; Joana slept in the first one with her daughters, the boys occupied the second. The side window overlooked the grove of cacao trees, from which I could see her during the classes, and be seen by her. There was never a better tended grove. I polished the ground with my boots; I think I even polished the trunks with the comings and goings of my shadow. She could have at least looked at the grove; but no, it was as if the window did not exist. In the afternoon, she would disappear; I am sure she was in the hallway fixing food for the following day. At dusk she shut everything up and picked up her crocheting. She never asked me for a kernel of corn, a haystraw. How did she manage to survive? Did she multiply the loaves, the fishes? Strange woman. I never understood her reckoning, she had the gift of multiplication. So did I, in my own way: that year I had two sons. But what I really wanted was to have one by Joana. I started to look for women who resembled her, could not find any, I spread the rumor around that I wanted to marry an educated woman. I remained ignored in my cacao grove. I decided to talk to the widow. She received me well: she saw I was flushed, offered me water, or coffee. How could I hold a glass, or a cup, when my hands were shaking? I did not utter a single word I had prepared. I had a hook in my tongue, I was mute, a fish. My father was never slighted when he mounted a half-blood horse he got in Bahia; with other horses or on the ground, his authority was lesser. Some things are like that, they make people stronger. I decided to move her to a larger house, where her system of support would perhaps weaken. "You're going to move this week. I'm going to pull this down, it's a good place to build a trading post. I need to increase my income. I've made many mistakes, but I'm going to straighten my life out, have a family." "You already have so many! One more is not going to make any difference." I pretended not to hear, left with my ears burning, gave orders to pull everything down, remove from my sight the window from which I had never been seen. I did not build anything in its place. The house I moved Joana to, along with the school and her children, was huge. It had been divided up: part of it was a distillery. Even so, a cry coming from the front room was barely heard in the kitchen. Damp walls, high ceilings, huge rooms that would accommodate six double beds and several dressers, and where on certain nights it was necessary to light a fire not to freeze to death. There, all at the same time, her children got sick, all of them, the younger one died. Her mother, who came to visit her from time to time, also died here. Nothing could break that woman. I spent three and a half years prowling about that house, only to lose my patience one day and walk right in to ask her, promising the moon, if she wanted to become my mistress. She did not answer. She looked me straight in the eyes, with her stern face. "Are you going to answer or not? Speak. What are you made of? Wood? Stone?" She kept staring. I decided to grab her once and for all, I wanted to see how far her haughtiness would go. I found myself walking in the cane brake, as if an invisible being had carried me off. This being, without any doubt, was my humiliation. The missionaries came. I confessed, had the five children who had been born to me in those five years baptized, decided to take the path of justice, took the teacher out of that big house, put her in an old stable. Partitions made of window blinds divided the space into rooms. I besieged her only to humiliate her, to destroy her pride, I obtained nothing. It is true that I did not speak to her, ever again, about going to bed with me. I complained, criticized her, insulted her, insisted on the evils of pride. Her answer, once: "Admittedly you speak from experience: you know what you're talking about." I decided to ask her to marry me. I did not have the courage to speak the words, not even when I found out that she was leaving. I hated her for years. I got women pregnant and loathed the children who were born, because none was *hers*. With time, my hatred began to fade, a kind of contentment took its place, gratitude, perhaps. I came to the conclusion that Joana Carolina had been my transcendence, my share of awe in a life so devoid of mystery.

SEVENTH MYSTERY

Those who spin and weave join and order dispersed materials
so that, otherwise, would be useless or nearly. They belong to
SPINNER THREAD SHEEP YARN the same lineage of geometri-
cians, they establish laws and points of union for what is separated. Before the spindle, **YARN WOOL FRAME COTTON YARN**
the distaff, the loom, before the inventions destined to extend
DISTAFF WEAVER BRAID YARN the threads and interlace them,
cotton, silk, it was as if they were still immersed in limbo, in the
night of formlessness. It is the call for order that brings them to
light, turns them into works **YARN LOOM SHEEP WEAVER YARN**
and thus into human creations, informed by the spirit of man. It
is not because they are useful to us that cotton or linen repre-
CROCHET SEWING LINEN YARN sent a victory of our intelli-
gence; but because they are woven, because an order sings in
them, the serene, the firm **YARN WARP PLAIT COCOON YARN**
and rigorous interlacing of the warp, of the woven threads. This
SPINNER THREAD SHEEP YARN is how their most noble expressions are those in which, with an even greater discipline,
the ornament flourishes: in **YARN SPIN WEAVE FABRIC YARN**
crochet, in a rug, in brocade. Then, it is as if by a sort of alchemy,
of algebra, of magic, cotton plantations and sheep, cocoons, fields
of flax, rose once again, with a less rebellious, but more lasting life.

◯ We did not even have an enema bag. My mother,
bending over, gives us a marshmallow root enema with
an ox bladder and a castorbean tube greased with pork
suet. We had a fever, our bodies were full of spots. We
ate very little, we were always prone to sickness. Be-

fore it had been whooping cough. We all coughed, Álvaro's skin burst below his ear. He was the one who suffered most. He had to take two cans of castor oil, two spoonfuls a day, with half an orange after each dose. He liked oranges, he wanted to eat a whole one; mother did not let him: it was too expensive. Everything was in half. Half an orange, half a loaf of bread, half a banana, half a glass of milk, half an egg, one shoe on and the other in the closet. We wore both only when she took us to town, to get her salary, three leagues one way and three back. The same way for almost eight years, never on horseback, by carriage or mule. Always on foot. In the beginning, she spoke to the important people. If they could give her a job closer to town. It was too far and there was no transportation. She could not come with all five children, she took one, or two, or three with her, the others stayed home, and that worried her. They frowned, shrugged. They told her to be patient. When possible…It was never possible. Mother let about three years pass without insisting on her request, going to town every month. Many hills, deserted stretches; places where you could not even hear a dog barking; stretches of sand, that tired you out more than the hills; an expanse full of rolling pebbles, which gleamed and wounded your feet. We used to cover our heads with straw hats in the summer. Who could stand to hold a parasol so long, however light it might be? The hats only kept our faces and necks from getting too sunburnt. And our brains from boiling. There came up from the ground—from the sand, the pebbles—an ardent breath that was difficult to swallow and blurred distances. A hot dust blew all over the place, it felt like salt, such was our thirst. And in certain stretches the trees fled, disbanded, and the only shade came from our hats. It was even worse when winter came. The swollen rivers did not always give way. And sometimes they did not and still we passed, because our need was great. Or we crossed them by means of rickety bridges, with the water roaring, licking our feet. One day Nô was almost gored by the horns of a dead bull, carried by the current. Everything turned to mud, so to speak. The wood of the bridges was muddy, the trees, the rivers were muddy masses advancing, and even the pebbles seemed to dissolve, become mud. Then—was there any other way?—we took umbrellas, held the handle with both hands, our fingers interlocked, and let our arms go dead. The winds came during the second part of the winter, a fast-growing plantation, sprouting with the first sudden downpours. They blew ceaselessly in that region. They hurt one's ears, turned umbrellas inside out, taking a single step became difficult, a laborious thing, every path turned into a hill. And we never came across decent men on the road: we only ran into drunks. Mother was afraid, I am sure of it. She had to be afraid, I know. She never showed it, except for one time. Only she and I had gone. We had arrived, as most other times, at dusk. Mother rested, got her money, sold some needlework; when she realized what time it was, it was already too late to go back. She decided to stay one more night, leave early in the morning. She got mixed up with hours and signals, thought that the moon was the morning coming, she woke me, we started for home. Already out of town, we saw that a man was following us. "It's going to be morning soon." It was not. Over her shoulder, mother watched the man and walked faster: so did he; she slowed down: the stranger slackened his step; mother stopped near a farm, a stable, never taking her eyes off the figure, pretending that our trip was over; our pursuer paused; we almost ran down a hill: when we looked back, we saw that the distance between him and us had changed very little. She said: "I was wrong about the time." Like someone who says: "I drank at the poisoned well." We had the night's poison in our bodies, without being able to vomit it, a poison of error, of abandon, of vulnerability. There was nobody on the road—and the man at our heels. All the way like that, until we arrived at the plantation. Then, she took me in her arms and ran. She was calling her sons aloud, with courage, like someone brandishing a weapon: they were names of men. The first light of day was beginning to appear from behind the hills. Nô came to open with a lamp in his hand, she rushed in with such force that she made him lose his balance, the glass chimney toppled between the three of us, shattered on the floor. The door locked, she sat down, asked for a glass of water. She was shaking from head to toe. Joy and abundance we only knew when my grandmother Totônia came from the town for a few days. Not that she was a cheerful person. Stern, spare of words, rarely smiling, her forehead lowered,

133

like a goat getting ready to butt. What other event, though, should we celebrate? Mother made cakes, sweets, she did not have to tell us twice to go out to the coconut trees and welcome her. All five of us went, the boys on foot, I on the back of the ram, Maria do Carmo on the sheep. Almost like brothers, those two animals: we talked to them, lived with them and, when it was very cold, they slept in bed with us. There were seven of us running toward our grandmother Totônia, shouting, when she emerged in a shawl, smock, long skirt, firm foot, speaking calmly, as if she were coming from just down the street and not from afar. She would arrive, once, to get sick and die within a few days, with the smell of the food mother had made to celebrate her visit still lingering in the house. At that time, there were only me, Téo and mother. Nô and Álvaro had left, gotten a job in a store, were starting their own life; Maria do Carmo, Carminha, sister beloved, my true companion, because she was a girl, had died of that illness whose name we did not know. It is to her that mother is giving the enema, with the oxbladder at the end of the castorbean tube. She resembles, my little sister, a grotesque glass-blower. The one with braids is me. Nô, Álvaro and Téo are not portrayed. But they were there, piled up with us in that room, all burning with fever. We had been forced to leave the house where we lived, move to this one in the forest: people with smallpox were sent there. We did not have smallpox. But we were lying in bed, all of us, sick with a serious illness that could spread. They told us to go. We went.

Right there, among the trees, Carminha was buried. In my fever I heard my mother digging the grave. The sheep bleated for a long time, a different kind of bleating, rueful—I had nightmares in which they had been bleating for seven years. During the our entire sickness our fare was bananas and coffee. There was an outbreak of bubonic plague in town, it was forbidden to go there, so the marshmallow root enemas were our only medicine. After this was over, mother started asking again for a job closer to town, only to hear the same refusals. And in this way eight more years passed, month after month, summers, winters, a month, then another, a year, another, under the sun, in the wind, mother crossing paths with drunks, running from mad dogs, wild oxen escaped from the corral, three leagues one way, three back, to get her pay for a whole month of work, from seven to two, every day, except Sundays only. Some say: *the time of childhood is a balmy April.* Mine was a windy and tormented August, which ended when, on a certain night, a black man with a face covered with warts came with a letter. "The daughter of the Queimadas plantation's owner thought of me, after all this time. They're going to open a school, her mother wants me to be the new teacher. They have an agent in town, I won't have to go there to get my salary." Tears were rolling out of my mother's tired eyes, worn from making crochet tablecloths by candlelight all those years in order to sell them in town. Only then did she confess: "I was so afraid of walking on those paths! Besides, each time I feel tireder. No matter how strong I try to be, my legs give out under me. I can't believe I won't have to take those trips any more." For the only time in all of her life, she raised her fist, an incredibly fragile fist, in a brief gesture of revolt against those roads traveled one hundred and eighty times. How could she hide her fear for so many years? The same black man with the face covered with warts took us to Queimadas. We went on horseback, Téo mad with joy, on a gray one, mother and I on a sorrel. Still within the boundaries of Serra Grande, on a knoll, she turned. From there we could see cane brakes and houses, the sugar mill's chimney, the water wheel, people, donkeys, goats, hens and horses, a stretch of the road we had walked so many times. I can hear her say: "I lived in this hell seven years, seven months and seven days. Seven years, seven months and seven days. It sounds like a sentence out of a book." She raised her open hand and wiped away the landscape, with the same gesture with which she erased from the blackboard what had already been taught and learned. For me, they had been ungodly years. But at that moment, realizing the end of a cycle and a world, I felt a pang coming from the depths of my memory. It was alongside the cemetery that we entered the town. We would get there, almost always, at six, seven. I was afraid of the crosses and hungry. I closed my eyes, not to see the graves, the will-o'-the-wisp, I walked like a blind person; and felt, with my whole being, the smell of coffee and bread enveloping the shacks, which for me was also a smell of rest, of respite, of streets, of safety, lights in the houses, the smell of the end of the journey. I suddenly missed those precarious moments. Avarice or zeal of our memory which, even among adversities, stores every grain of calm weather in its saddlebag.

Eighth Mystery

The black soil, the sugar cane, the Cayenne cane, the purple cane, the demerara crystals, the sugar candy, the mill, the spout, the syrup, the boiler, the distillery, the rum, the sugar, the field hand, the mill worker, the overseer, the chief, the master, the first harvest, the second harvest, the planting, the replanting, the rake, the plow, the ox, the horse, the wagon, the wagoner, the turnplow, the furrow, the graft, the hole, the winter, the summer, the floods, the drought, the manure, the bagasse, the clearing, the hoeing, the scythe, the cutting, the ax, the knife, the crushing, the crusher, the counting, the trading post, the fence, the sluice, the hoe, the rifle, the cooperation, the servitude, the killer, the protector, the underling, the boss.

⊕ Totônia on the bed, her eyes closed, her hands on the sheet. The Bull's head, with its curved horns, nearly fills the window frame. I bend over the sick woman with a tin basin in my hands. At the foot of the bed (the three of them forming a kind of fleury cross) Lucina on her knees, dressed in white, Suzana behind her, in blue, with her fists raised and, behind the group, also kneeling, Filomena, whose open arms with their puffy red sleeves alone are visible. On the left, Joana Carolina, prostrated, touches the wooden floor with her forehead and the palms of her hands. From the open door, Laura is watching us. Shining through the walls and over the countryside, the clear May day and the undulations of the land, above which fly big white birds, their lovely heads adorned with a horn, their wings weighed down by the light. There is the rider on the trail, the boy, all alone, and the covered wagon, pulled by four oxen, the rear team red, the front one purple. The driver has a black flag tied to the end of his switch, on horseback are Nô and Álvaro, summoned by Joana; the boy traveling alone, Teófanes, is taking a letter to the pharmacist; we are in the wagon, with the dead woman. Her idea, which I opposed, was to wait until a herdsman appeared, or a young man at least, to escort the two of us. In the middle of the corral, far away from any trees, the Bull unexpectedly leaped at us with its horns. We threw ourselves down, our faces pressed against the manure-covered ground, protecting our heads, the Bull kicked her purse away, tried to gore her in the back with its horns, I wanted to get up, scream, scare it off, I had no voice, or courage, or legs, the man on horseback appeared, wearing a hat and sideburns, drove the animal away, got off, spoke, smiled and took us by the arm. To the other side of the fence. To think that I almost kissed his claws, unaware that he carried hidden under his coat the beasts of evil, with their shod hooves, their sharp horns! During the four days of

Totônia's agony, Joana's house filled with people. To be precise, he was the only one who did not show up. He and his father, who had lost his mind and spent his days on the porch, in his nightshirt, swinging in the hammock and scouring pans with sand. The son, had he been someone else, would have come, he was the Bull's master. Totônia, it is true, arrived as if nothing had happened, ate Joana's cakes, recited the litanies and the rosary. It was not until later that she began to get weak, became paralyzed on one side, even though she did not have any wounds. But it was apparent, she was wasting away because of what she had gone through in the corral. After I washed the dead woman and put her best dress on her (darned at the hem), Joana gave me her instructions. Totônia abhorred the idea of surrendering her mortal remains to strange soil, it was necessary to take her corpse home and bury her among inscriptions with familiar names, which she might have heard with dislike, or loathing, during her life, but were part of her world. Joana wanted a wagon, to borrow or to rent. The man asked if I was a member of the family. "By the color of my skin, you can see that I'm not." "Then by what right are you coming?" "I'm coming as a friend. In the same basin in which I washed the deceased, I gave all of her children their first bath." "That's no right. Tell the teacher to come herself." He shouted, seeing me at Joana's side, for me to wait outside, he did not allow blacks in the chapel. It was in the chapel, right next to the plantation house, that he shut the door, slamming it loudly. He did not even seem the

same person who had saved us from the Bull, he must
be having a bad day, that is what I thought. Everything
was so quiet! The hammock on the porch, the creaking
of the hooks, slow, the father unhurriedly scouring the
copper pans. I pricked up my ears to hear what was
going on in the chapel. I did not grasp the meaning of
all that show. Was all that necessary for what we were
asking? Then the calm broke and I heard. The man's
words, the outrageous price. How dared he voice such
a brutal demand in front of the saints? I waited for
Joana's protestations, cries of anger. I could only hear
her voice, which was not even tearful, a monotonous
voice, word after word, all the same. Then the man's
tone lowered and Joana's remained unchanged. There
was a bang, a kick on the wooden floor or a knock
against the door, and the voices ceased. Until the man's
rose again, loud and plaintive at the same time, shouting his conditions. "Just say yes or no. Right now!" Joana
was going to answer. Maybe I should have stayed, found
out everything, coped with the situation. In the middle
of the corral, the Bull in front of us, I remained suspended, with no ground under my feet, discovering in
myself a sense of growing helplessness, a feeling of
despair eating me up. I felt the same now: within the
silence, some monster turned its dark horns against
me. I did not have the courage to wait for the answer,
ran up on the porch, next to the old man and his folly,
where for a moment I felt safe. Joana came out, I did
not ask her if she had managed to get the wagon. We
walked back without exchanging a word, together only

in body, our souls elsewhere; the house full of people and her sisters in tears, but keeping their purse strings tight; Joana sitting, her eyes dry, staring at the floor, her hands between her knees, I standing in front of her, two hours, three, until a piercing, moaning noise was heard, drawing closer. I saw the top of the wagon, the driver's switch, with the black rag tied to it. Joana said: "Let's take our mother away. She's going to rest where she wanted." "For your mother, you did what you could and what you couldn't. God bless you." I tried to dissuade her, when she sent the boy to town for medicines: "Don't waste your money, this illness can't be cured." "How do you know?" "It's like recognizing a prostitute, or a man who used to be a priest: something imperceptible, that you feel more than see." "I don't think she'll make it either. But it is a law of mine, to always act as if nothing were impossible." In the room, the basin in my arms, bending over Totônia to give her a hot footbath, I curse the brutish animal that destroyed her and think how, in this world, like the rest of us, she lived like someone in the middle of a cattle stampede, surrounded by horns, gored by horns. In the wagon, accompanying her, now dead, and listening to the wooden wheels creaking in the axletrees, I see things in a different light, I have the impression of going, with her, toward God, in a wagon pulled by oxen with great wings, half angels, half oxen, oxen-angels, and that in the world, life and people, and maybe even God, are oxenangels, and that, of every thing, we have to eat, with our weak teeth, some horn, some wing.

NINTH MYSTERY

W O R D C Twice was the world created: when it evolved from nothing-
A P I T A ness to existence; and when, elevated to a more subtle plan,
L P A L I it became word. Chaos, therefore, did not cease with the
M P S E S appearance of the universe; but when the conscience of man,
T C A L L naming the creation, and thus recreating it, separated, or-
I G R A P dered, united. The word, however, is not the symbol or
H Y H I E reflection of what it signifies, a subordinate function, but
R O G L I rather its spirit, the breath on the clay. A thing does not
P H I C Q really exist until it is named: then, it becomes invested with
U I L L C the word which illuminates it and, achieving identity, also
O D E X B acquires stability. Because no twin is like the other; only the
O O K P A word **twin** is really identical to the word **twin**. Thus, innu-
R C H M E merable twin of itself, the word is what remains, the center,
N T A L P the invariable, untainted by the fluctuation surrounding it
H A B E T and saving what was said from the transformations that would
P A P E R end up by negating it. Evocative to the point that a place, a
S T O N E kingdom, never disappears completely, as long as the name
S T Y L U designating it (Byblos, Carthage, Sumeria), the word, being
S I L L U the spirit of what—even though only imaginarily—exists, still
M I N A T remains, because incorruptible, like the splendor of what was,
I O N W R capable, even when forgotten, of being restored to its original
I T I N G clarity. It differentiates, fixes, orders and recreates: the word.

⊘ The two of us arm in arm, our faces close together, we seem to be both looking at each other and
ahead of us. Behind us, sideways, with crossed necks,
one tail on the left and the other on the right, white,

thick, sweeping the ground like wedding gowns, our two horses. Shining above us, two stars, large and red. △ One above Miguel's head: it looks like a rose. ○ The other above Cristina's : it looks like a pomegranate. ◉ We are the lovers, the fugitives, the persecuted, the discovered, the saved. We did not know which way to go, how our journey would end. We wanted to leave without knowing where to go, be happy if only for one day, sleep somewhere, not think about the time approaching, even though we knew that there was someone coming after us, ○ Cristina's father's men, we did not know how many, tracking us down, certainly armed. △ It was not likely that my father would order his thugs to kill me; but Miguel would not escape. To run away with me, the daughter of Antônio Dias! ○ That is right, to elope with her, the only daughter of the great Antônio Dias, the owner of three plantations who, after his wife died, did not remarry so that all his wealth would belong to her, without any divisions or shares! △ That was not the reason, it was out of wisdom, mother was a woman of caliber; difficult to find her qualities in a second wife. ○ That is what you say, not the people; Antônio Dias, with the land of those three plantations, tried to bury your life, marry you off to whomever he wanted. △ All right, then. ◉ Because his name was Antônio, on the twelfth of June he gathered friends and relatives, killed pigs, bullocks and turkeys, built fires as tall as a horse, had scores of men shoot their blunderbusses in the air, △ had pans of canjica corn custard, corn pudding, corn on the cob, peanut brittle, rusks, meringues, tapioca cakes made, fired girandoles of a hundred and twenty skyrockets, ◐ ordered casks of green wine, invited singers, released balloons with the name of the Saint and of the three old-fashioned sugar mills, hired the best accordionists, the dance started before seven, went on throughout the night and early morning and ended when the sun was high. When it was all over, he lowered the banner of his patron from the pole, fired the last girandole and went to sleep for twenty-four hours. △ It was during this interval that we eloped. I told one of the black women I was going for a ride and, still wearing my holiday dress, got on my horse, went to meet Miguel. ◯ I waited without believing that she would come; it may even be that I wished some difficulty would keep her from coming. I had my small farm, a good little life; and even though all I wanted in the world was to join myself, come what may, to Ana Cristina, I was afraid, like all men, of the greatness, I was frightened by that space that all of a sudden opened up for me and that could swallow me in its light. △ I saw this fear in Miguel's face, asked him if he wanted to give up. He answered: "Even if I wanted, I would no longer be able to, now. Your beauty is compelling me." I do not know whether my beauty could force someone like that, but I accepted his words and felt in me, in my face, a splendor, there was something in me that could make a man give up his security and pursue adventure, rise above all the dead hours of his life and burn, in one minute, the useless wealth accumulated until then. I spurred my horse, rode on, he cried out my name: "Do you know what you're doing?" "Don't ask me any more questions. From now on, I want everything to be an answer." ◎ We rode on, at each other's heels. We flew through the fields, gaining distance, counting on the old man's sleep, but knowing that they could wake him any time, and that he would come after us with his men without any trouble, guided by the reports of those who saw us going like the wind, looking like criminals running from the law. It did not take them long to go to the plantation house, eager to inform him of what had happened. They could not get him out of bed before six, when, being the middle of the year and cloudy, it was already very dim. He thought he was dreaming, was it a nightmare?, he splashed water on his face, asked them to repeat their story. "Set fire to the farm and get six horses ready." He named those who would go with him after us, all men who could see a footprint in the wind, who could follow an animal by its smell, men who had never lost the trail of an ox, however faint it might have been, who not even horse thieves could trick. How could we hope to escape them? He was already in the saddle, when he changed his mind: "I'm not going. It's not right for a father to go around the world after his daughter like this. She's the one who has to come to me." "What about the man?" "You already know what to do with him." At this time, from

Igaraçu to Afogados da Ingarazeira, and from Coururipe to Flores, like a sagging hammock that stretched all the way to Santana de Ipanema, a storm to end all storms came down and washed out our tracks. We were coming into a ghost town, with trees already growing in the middle of the streets, branches crowding inside doors and windows. It was a windy place and almost all the ceilings had collapsed, the beams had rotted, the remaining ridgepoles were giving under the weight of the roofs. There were toads, scorpions and perhaps snakes hidden inside the houses which were rotting and already starting to take on the color of dirt and leaves. We called out, and when we realized that the two of us were the only living creatures there, advancing (among crooked windows, ruined walls and battered-in doors) on our exhausted horses, there arose in our souls a happiness bigger than the farm and the three plantations together, bigger than Pernambuco and Alagoas, bigger than Bahia, and we kissed in our saddles, so inflamed with love that our bodies, like the horses', steamed in the rain. We got off, walked on with our arms around each other, leading our horses by the reins, without knowing what to do with ourselves and our happiness. We got to a square where the church was. The portal gave, we went in with the horses, their hooves clattered on the mosaic. We called out again, nobody answered. We took off our clothes and soon knew each other, on top of a pine chest, while the horses, hungry, standing in the open door, watched the night falling. If we brought them in, it was not out of disrespect, sacrilege. We were afraid that our pursuers would discover us thanks to them. But we did not make a gesture, not a word did we say to hold them back, when—after the rain—they went out in search of pasture. We saw them going out very well. Should we, then, interrupt our caresses, go out after them and thus undo that heavy certainty, born in us, that nothing in the world could break up our delightful embrace? And even though we were hungry, since we had finished our provisions during the long journey, we stayed on the chest, sleeping and making love, our bodies worn out by the ride, aching if we turned, if we separated. When we heard the horse shoes on the pavement of the church at night, we thought they were our pursuers and believed our time had come. The moon was shining in through the open door, the skylights and some holes. We opened the chest to hide inside it, it was full of human bones. At this point, the horses appeared, they were ours, we decided to continue our journey. Still kissing, we put on our wet clothes. Before leaving, we knelt, hand in hand, before the altar of Saints Cosme and Damian, △ I raised my face, exclaimed: "I take this man as my husband, before you and God, not for a part of eternity, but for all eternity: his name is Miguel." ○ I also raised my voice in the silence, taking the horses as witnesses and shaking from head to toe, because I had the impression that hundreds of souls were witnessing our wedding: "I take this woman whose name is Ana Cristina, without any of her earthly belongings, as my wife, for all of my life." ⊘ Each of us made the gesture of slipping a ring on the other's finger. We got back on the road without a clear direction, the wedding rings on our left hands, as visible and real as the love that guided, or misguided, us. We crossed rivers, fell into fish traps, swapped horses with a band of gypsies, bought new clothes at a fair, three times we recognized places we had passed through before, slept on our saddles, in the woods, under a bridge, cried in each other's arms. Neither of us knew where we were going. Our destination, at that time, was not a direction, a place, a town, a house, our destination was to go. Or at least so we thought, until we arrived, more dead than alive, at the Queimadas plantation and knocked on the door of Dona Joana Carolina, at that time entering her Winter. As soon as she saw us, she understood everything, so that we did not have to tell her our story. Stern, she smiled at us with her eyes, took us in, made all the provisions hospitality calls for. When she asked us questions, it was as if she already knew almost everything: when we were expecting our pursuers, if they would come on friendly terms or armed. "We don't know." "The owner of the plantation, here, likes everybody to visit her at night under the pretext of chatting. Actually, it's to husk her corn and shell her beans. Aside from that, she's a good person. But don't count on her, she never meddles in other people's business." "What about you?" We asked because we recognized the mark of compassion in her, she was for us someone who had been awaiting our coming, with our effigies in hand, carved by someone who knew us, so as to avoid mistakes. The answer was the one we had been hoping for: "I'll do what I can: I, too, have loved." We slept in separate rooms, soaking up the comforting smell of clean sheets. The pillowcases smelled of oranges. We woke up surrounded by children, eager to see the fugitives, the sweethearts, the newcomers. It was a day of clouds and fine rain. We talked little. Surrendering without any resistance to Joana's wise and experienced look, without perceiving her presence in our intimacy, within our walls, as an invasion, but rather as the disciplined arrival of well armed men, amicable and grave, to protect them. We were becoming, as the hours passed, more aware of ourselves, stronger. At ten at night, the group we had been expecting surrounded the house. We remained in Joana's own room, with the girl and her brother, over whose heads we looked at each other, secretly blaming ourselves for having involved that poor family in our folly, and at the same time believing that we had been led blindly unto the only person in the world who could save us. Joana made the chief get off his horse, invited him in, spoke to him firmly: "These two children have been roaming around for almost a week, sustained only by their love. This is worth a great deal. I've been working for years without anyone's help to support my children. How, then, can I bear to see this girl forced to flee without even taking with her, out of all her riches, something she could hold in the palm of her hand, following an impulse, only because her father won't listen to her? Is that a father? I know very well that money is important. But compassion is greater. What's the use of having cattle and plantations if you can't find some magnanimity in your heart?" She argued for over two hours, until she obtained from the chief the promise that he would protect us and would only turn us in if our wedding were permitted. Then we left. Those who had been our persecutors were now friends, our guardians, repeating Joana's words to themselves with a wonder magnified by the early morning. △ The splendor of certain human works is lasting, lingering like a halo, even when nobody in the world is capable of reconstituting them. What Joana had said, albeit poorly repeated, silenced my father. At last he had found someone who talked to him with authority and justice, as my mother had always done. ◯ He immediately set up a date for the wedding, and three days later he wrote a letter asking for Joana's hand. He sent it by four bearers, he wanted to emphasize the seriousness of his intentions. The short reply: "Not even if I had an entire life at my disposal could I make you or anyone else realize to what extent the now distant time of my marriage brightens my days, however dark they may be. In truth, having consecrated myself to my husband for my entire life, I remain faithful to him. I am therefore very honored by your kind and generous offer. It would mean, if I accepted it, shelter and stability for the rest of my days. But, then, what would become of my soul?"

TENTH MYSTERY

The polar icecaps, the temperate zones and the ring of the equator, still exhaling the hot breath of the anvils. Continents and islands, steely peaks, plains, mountain chains, valleys, dunes, sea cliffs, promontories. What lies, invisible, under our feet: columns, forgotten gods, porticoes, ancestral tibias, minerals, fossils, silent empires. Earthquakes, volcanoes. The mud, the turf, the flowers, the shrubs, the centenary trees, wood and fruit, the shade of their boughs. The terrestrial animals. The revolving of the seasons within a greater season, entire civilizations blossoming and dying in one vast Autumn, in one Winter of millenniums.

(Joana, a saw in her hand, is cutting off the legs of the wooden bench where the boy sleeps, with a blue paper boat on his chest. Seated, he thanks Joana, with his face in the shadows, by offering her the boat.) 1. "What was the name of this boy?" 2. "Maximino, apparently. Or Raimundo. But some say Glaura, or Glória, who knows?" 3. "He must have been a horse thief, to have so many names." ⊕ "He was just a child and he couldn't walk, there was something wrong with his legs."

3. "When someone is born crippled, it's because God has put an obstacle in the path of his wickedness. I never knew a blindman who was any good." 4. "You say these things, but you aren't bad. What spills out of the mouth has no place in the heart." (He could walk, with some help. He spent his days in a chair, at the window, watching the passers-by. He made paper boats and his name was Jonas. He was fourteen, but looked eleven.) 1. "Did Joana always go there?" ⊕ "Once in a while. She didn't go anywhere 'always.' That day, she only went to saw the bench." 3. "There couldn't be anything so special about that cripple, to make some-one go there to save him because of a vision. He wasn't a saint, nor a family man. A useless creature." 4. "Maybe it wasn't him that God wanted Joana to save, but the criminal, preventing him from murdering an innocent." 2. "The malefactor came to kill someone, sent by God knows whom. I don't know how many deaths he had on his conscience." ⊕ "Maybe it was precisely him that Our Lord wanted to save." (It was the month of Saint Anne and it was raining fairly hard that afternoon. So, it seems really strange that Joana Carolina, even though she did not live far, would go to Floripes' house. She used to visit her often, since she had first heard about her ill fortune: her mother's plantation sold at a public auction, her unhappy marriage, after an engagement of fourteen years, her crippled son. Not when the weather was bad, though; in this case, since she had moved back into town, thanks to Nô and Álvaro, she

liked to sit on the sofa, listening to the rain. When she heard what had happened to Jonas, she was happy, but did not give any sign of believing in a revelation, a warning: "I sawed off the legs of that bench because I was afraid. Jonas could have fallen off and gotten hurt. The bench is too narrow for a sick child.") 2. "The stepmother, or aunt, the woman who was living with the kid, moved in with a cousin, or to an institution. Or was it some nephew who went to live with her." ⊕ "This story of aunts and stepmothers is a fabrication. The child lived with his mother." 1. "Who was she?" 2. "She came from some wealthy family and, nobody knows how, all of a sudden she became very poor." 3."She certainly didn't do anything good, to end up that way. She must have led a dissolute life, when she was young. I bet the kid was the son of Joana's brother, the one who disappeared. I bet he ended up in jail." 2. "I heard that João had gotten married somewhere, to somebody's widow, I don't remember her name. It was foreign. And that this widow had inherited I don't know how many thousands. I'm not quite sure whether it was this João or another." 3. "Some French whore, for sure." ⊕ "He didn't even get married, nor was the boy his. The woman's name was Floripes and she was the daughter of the former owner of the Queimadas plantation. At that time, she already had the voice and the posture of an old woman. But her face was still very young, and pretty." 4. "Old age is like a crab, we don't all age in the same way. It gradually stretches out its claws inside us. At times it starts from the back, others from the legs, others from the head. In my case, it began from the dreams: I started to dream almost every night about people from my past." (In Joana, that crab stretched out its claws in one stroke. It hit her kidneys and her face, her joints, her teeth and memory, her digestive tract, her hearing, her sleep, snatched almost all of her friends, took Nô and Álvaro, dead before their mother, seized Suzana, Filomena, Lucina, it struck her in almost every possible way. But Laura and Teófanes, married, lived nearby and took care of her. She had enough bread, meat and milk, a new pair of shoes at the end of the year, she had her things, did not need to work any more. Unlike those who focus on their miseries and remain insensitive to all kinds of good things, Joana was content with what was left to her. She admitted that she had had her share of suffering, adding with resignation that a long life is always accompanied by a great deal of pain, and that it is a lack of respect to lament our losses, oblivious to the good side of things.) 3. "There are people who die with delusions of grandeur. That Floripes, just because of who her mother was, I heard that she always snubbed those who lived with her in the tenement." ⊕ "It was a big house, not a tenement. In the room where she slept with the boy, there was a door nailed shut, to separate it from a kind of sitting room, in which all kinds of people lived. The boy slept up against this door. You know: children toss around a lot." 3. "Only when they have worms." ⊕ "The boy would bang against the door all night long, with his elbows." 1. "And is it true that, when his mother, that Floripes, died, it turned out that she kept golden diadems, platinum brooches, necklaces, earrings, bracelets, bangles, valuable objects hidden in a box?" 2. "Some say so." (At first she had kept these things with her out of insecurity. She wanted to be sure that in case of extreme necessity she would have somewhere to turn for assistance. But, while she talked ceaselessly about her years of abundance, she thought that she could endure the many hardships a little longer, until the day when, having decided to sell one of the pieces, she could not find the courage to do so, fearing that people would guess there was more. Joana suspected the existence of these jewels. And all her conversations with Floripes revolved around the idea that if we do not take advantage of our present wealth it becomes even more distant than all the possessions and benefits of the past.) 3. "Poor kid. He lived like a convict, sleeping on a bench, without a pillow, I bet, thanks to his mother. That woman should have sold the gold and taken care of her son. Avarice is a plague." 4. "Every man for himself and God for all. Nobody is alone. Think about the bench. It was more important for the boy than being healthy." 1. "But is it really true? How did Joana know? How did she guess?" (Whenever it rained Jonas was in pain, his joints hurt. That is why Joana went there with the saw that winter afternoon. She wanted to clear up the business of

Floripes' box once and for all, saw it open if necessary. When the time came, though, she did not have the courage to bring that matter up, and that is why she shortened the legs of the bench.) 3. "Can you believe it? That a man would kill just because the boy banged against the door. And to shoot without even knowing who's on the other side!" 4. "His crime wouldn't have been any lesser if he had known." (There were four shots, each about a hand's width apart, exactly at the level the boy would have been, if it had not been for Joana's intervention.) 1. "And what about that terrible man, how did he end up?" 2. "At that time, he had already killed who knows how many people. When he heard about the miracle, he put up his guns. He became something or other, I don't know what, I don't remember where."

Eleventh Mystery

What is it, what is it? Lion of invisible teeth, of tooth he is made and bites with his mane, with his tail, with his entire body. He does not cast a shadow on the ground; and the shadows flee when he is present, even though they are, of all that exists, the only thing his wrath and hunger will spare. His skin, hotter than that of bears and camels, and even the other lions', warms us from afar. Unlike other animals, he may be born without a father, without a mother: he is begotten, at

times, by two flints. Even though he devours everything, denying nothing to his molars, canines and inci-
sors, he symbolizes life. Easily domesticated in captiv-
ity, he is fierce when loose and in prides. Nothing en-
rages him more than the wind.

✝ In the old iron bed, the flame of her life about to
go out, in her right hand a handful of feathers and in
the left a dry tree branch, she confesses her sins to me.
Two angels are keeping vigil, one solemn, the other
smiling. On the roof, horses are galloping. The winds
of August. Horses were galloping on the roof tiles. At
my side, the chrism, the crucifix, a sliced lemon, a dish
with six raw cotton bolls. When she saw me, she
grabbed my arm. "I remember when you came here
last. It was almost supper time. I was putting some water
on the fire, was about to make coffee." I cultivate the
habit of forgetting. A priest must protect himself from
the infiltration of things. And what other human blessing is more insidious than memories with their two-
sided nature, bringing us simultaneously the joy of
possession and the sorrow of loss, one the reflection
of the other? Think of the warning of St. John of the
Cross, according to whom our memory centers on God
only to the extent that the soul unburdens it of the
things which, important as they may be, are not God
himself. How can we reach perfection in this sense,
though? At Joana's words, that afternoon, a kind of
nitrous gush, a salty vomit came up my throat. The

afternoon she spoke of was a peaceful experience, unique in every aspect. I saw the past as if in a mirror, Joana moving on the other side of the glass, with her fire and her song, but not on this side: behind me, absence. There would never be another afternoon like that, the Angel of Death was beckoning to Joana. "Father: I tried all my life to live in justice. Do you think I succeeded?" "Without a doubt." "He who talks a lot makes many mistakes. We can keep from talking; but not from living. I've lived eighty-six years. I must have made so many mistakes!" "That's part of our condition." "I know." In the prolonged silence, during which her hand was still clutching my arm, she was reviewing her actions, all those she could remember. She wanted to discover, among those she had begun or consummated during her long life, a blemish, an essential fallacy to confess to me and thus not appear proud. "Father, many times I've wanted to kill." It was as if she were bragging, as if her absolution depended on this, on this lie told with effort and timidity. "I must have committed injustices too. I must have. I can remember almost nothing by now. Neither the evil I did, nor that which I suffered. Now everything is almost of one color. Isn't this the way the world is, at…" She let my arm go, made a gesture with her hand, as if she were putting out a light or a flame, which doubtlessly meant: "…at dusk?" "I'm afraid, father." Her voice, fading, was like an old corroded instrument, a clarinet full of lichens and spiderwebs. It was difficult for her to put together those last few words, as if she were writing them out. She looked away, became still, staring at the rooftiles, distant. Her white hair, thick, was strewn on the pillow on both sides of her face. I thought that Joana Carolina was finally going to rest in God and prayed aloud, with renewed fervor. Then through her wrinkles, through her strewn hair, I saw her in her youth. Could it be possible that our soul has the opportunity to choose, among the countless faces we have lost, the least contrary to its nature, or that which witnessed our richest days, those in which we were closest to the always desired harmony between our power and our deeds? Could it have been that privileged face, resurrected from some distant plenitude, that I contemplated with piety and awe? Her old woman's features remained intact, with her dim eyes, the countless wrinkles. But within this face, which suddenly took on an inexplicable transparency, as if it really did not exist, as if it were a crust of deceit over a reality kept from ordinary contemplation, shone Joana's face at twenty, with a fire, a rapture and a nobility that seemed to defy life and its stigmas—and I was able to see that secret beauty, already forgotten by all those who had beheld it in the past, and that surfaced then on the eve of death, by the grace of God, before my eyes from which for a second the scales with which we go through life had fallen. The day before, she had divided among her closest relatives what she deemed to be, according to her modest standards, her wealth, the inheritance: a

quilt with a white and brown pattern, a set of silverware for five with wrought handles, two bath towels
never used, a plaster statuette. Having always lived
among hardships, these were her luxuries. It did not
occur to her to give anyone the dresser, the china closet,
the tables, the chairs, furniture she had always lived
with and which, incorporated into her daily existence,
did not seem to her to have any value, at least not a
value that could be dissociated from herself, rather,
she viewed them as a part of her own being, leveled
with it and insignificant in the same way; while the
unusual silverware, or the quilt with boughs and lions,
things she could not imagine existing during the winters in which her children took the sheep to bed, must
have seemed luxurious to her, desired by everybody
to the extent that she herself, in her poverty, had lacked
such sober splendors. Seeing her (or should I say s*ee-
ing them,* for I held before my eyes two different beings, both real and made one by my fear alone?), seeing her filled with the internal clarity of this new image, the mystery of the spirit or of the flesh, resurrected from a past no one would dare imagine tan-
gible, I thought she had saved for me, without knowing it, another kind of legacy, the privilege to witness,
on her death bed, that fleeting resurrection, more dis-
quieting than that of the dead, the return of a face to
the face it had turned into, of a youth devoured by
time and still transcending it, free, for a second, of its
somber entrails. When I anointed her with the chrism,

that preterit face had already vanished, and only its remnants, its dust, were left. It was over her eyes, her mouth, her ears, her old woman's hook nose, that I invoked the mercy of God. Even so, leaving that house I did not feel in my soul the weight of old age and death, which many times until then—and even after—had affected my priestly silences. Something shone in the heart of these phenomena, a sentence, a word, a semblance, something complete and at the same time veiled, as the form announced, surmised, still unrevealed, still unconquered must be for an artist. Inside me, as I walked away with my head high, Joana burned like a flame. *Populus, qui ambulabat in tenebris, vidit lucem magnam.*

FINAL MYSTERY

∞ The group of houses, the crosses, birds and trees, cows and horses, the road, the windmills, us taking Joana to the cemetery. We, Montes-Arcos, Agostinhos, Ambrósios, Lucas, Atanásios, Ciprianos, Mesateus, Jerônimos, João Crisostómos, João Orestes, we. Hats in our hands, hard faces, rough hands, denim clothes, leather sandals, we, greengrocers, market vendors, butchers, carpenters, middlemen in the cattle business, saddlers, sellers of fruit and birds, men of uncertain means and without a future, are taking Joana to the cemetery, we, the nobodies of this town, because the

others, the people with money and power, always ignored her. Joana, in her best dress (white honeysuckle
with foliage on a gray background), her shoes old but
still new (they walked so little), her sagging stockings,
the rosary with which she prayed her entire life for
those she loved and those who persecuted her. Streets
and roofs, walls, crosses, trees, euphorbia hedges, red
clay. The world that was hers, to which we have returned and which some of us never left, the land where
we eat, make love, curse, sweat and are annihilated,
always thinking of leaving and never going, who knows
why. Women at the windows, old men on the sidewalks, girls arm in arm, young men on street corners,
children in the square (Áureos and Marias, Beneditos
and Neusas, Chicos and Ofélias, Dalvas and Pedros,
Elzas and Quintinos) watch the funeral pass among
the houses of blue, green, red and yellow pediments, it
is an early September morning, end of winter, the trees
fully in leaf, and the sky divided in two seasons, white
clouds on one side, storm clouds on the other, a blue
and calm river between these two banks. To end her
days during which almost everything was scarce, as it
still is for us, drinking anything became very difficult
for Joana Carolina. She dreamed about fountains and
water spouts, and her only ambition those last days
was to drink a jug of water, savoring every swallow.
She resigned herself to moistening her lips and gums
with cotton soaked in milk. Now, with the white, green
and gray dress she used to wear on Sunday afternoons,

and enveloped by the silence that was her only companion, we are taking her to the cemetery. This is not the first coffin we take, nor will it be the last, we have already carried many, important dead or poor ones like us, from Lakes to Brookes, from Rocks to Cliffs, from Hills to Moores, from Clays to Beryls, but we never had such a strong and disturbing feeling that this was the ark of the Next Great Flood, that the new vengeful waters would fall upon us for forty days and forty nights, drowning even the snakes and the fish, and that only Joana would survive, to give birth with a gesture to the creatures she pleased: plants, animals, Javans, Magogs, Togarmahs, Ashkenazes. How many times was the world sterile and blinding for her, a city of salt, with houses of salt, salty fountains and avenues of salt? How many times was taking one step forward, living one more year, day, instant, like walking on sharp knife blades? How many times did her life seem like a river during the first rains, full of uprooted trees, of water lilies from the weirs and stillwaters, coiling around her hands and feet, getting into her mouth? And she always managed to catch a glimpse in the end, through the meshes of blindness, to balance on the edge of the cutting steel, disentangle herself from the waters, from the perplexities. We are taking her to the cemetery, amidst the cawing and the barking, the roosters crowing, the pigs grunting, moos, neighs, wind in the mangoes, children calling, cries, washerwomen's songs. She asked her daughter: "What month is this?" Her fear of death was gone. This meant that death was preparing for its leap. "September? Then it's not far." She said that two girls very much alike, clothed in white, had called her. Out of their feet grew a long vertical stem, with a lily at its end, enormous, floating next to their faces. They gave her an olive branch and a big lead fishhook. "Come, there will be three of us." They put an ermine cape on her shoulders. She tore the cape off, planted the branch, did not know what to do with the fishhook. The three of them ran out, through rocky tunnels. The girls were light, Joana heavier. Suddenly, they found themselves near a fire. Standing, looking at it in silence, her arms hanging, Totônia seemed to be lost in thought. Two feet from her old head, a little to the left and as if suspended by threads, hung an iron disk. Iron, we say. Joana was praying, she took it between her fingers. But everything on earth had lost its weight. Everything. Except her body. Surprised, she called her mother, could not hear her own voice, her mother did not turn, she ran out and saw the moon, in the middle of the day, with a dark ring around it, moving through space at great speed. Crazy moon. The luminous parts, when they passed through the clouds, became brighter, an intense and blinding clarity. The earth was white, the ground and the plants, the shadows on the ground, everything was white, immaculate earth. The moon disappeared below the horizon. And everybody saw that the whiteness of the world was just a crust, a skin that was cracking, cracked, dissolved, laying bare the splendor and the dirt of the grove of trees, of the ground, the color of the world. Rose-apples, pink mangoes, cashews, guavas, pomegranates, everything was hanging from the branches, it was an abundance, an orchard generous and laden with scents, Joana and the two girls began to run, now on the prairie, hand in hand. A green pasture, full of sheep and shady trees. Suddenly, her dead ones, invisible, began to call. Álvaro was calling Nô, Nô was calling Maria do Carmo, she was calling her sister, her sister Totônia, Totônia Jerônimo, Jerônimo Nô, Nô Filomena, Filomena Lucina, Lucina Floripes, Floripes Jerônimo, Jerônimo Suzana, Suzana Totônia, and Totônia was calling Saros. "I don't know who Saros was. But I felt proud to be the mother of so many dead and a widow, of not dying a virgin, of having given birth to you all. Are we in September?" "Yes." "The time is near. I smell lime, cement, moss. September, you said?" "Yes." We are carrying Joana to the cemetery, crossing the town and its smell of stables, of virgin wax, of spilled milk, of sweat, of fruit, of cut timber, of damp walls, among Floras and Ruis, Glórias and Sálvios, Hélios and Teresas, Isabels and Ulisses, Josés and Veras, Luízas and Xerxes, Zebinas and Áureos. She lived her life with meekness and justice, humility and firmness, love and compassion. She died with reduced possessions and lessened friends. Never did the plundering of others unleash any ambitions in her soul. Never did the evil suffered engender in her soul other evils. She died at the end of the winter. Will another like her be born in the next season? The white, the green, the gray. White walls, cypresses, somber gravestones. Beneath the ground, beneath the plaster, beneath the lizards, beneath the weeds, the silent guests appear. Hawthornes and Myrtles, Hazels and Olives, Rosewoods and Laurels. They dressed them—why this pointless generosity?— in their Sunday suits, the finest dress, the best tie, the newest shoes. Strange reunion: all with their lips sealed, hands crossed, heads bare, all stiff, their eyelids closed and all facing the same direction, as if waiting, all alone, in front of a big portico through which someone was about to pass. A judge, an admiral, a harpist, a waiter with trays. Bringing what? Salt, ashes, absinthe? Teeth, mold, slime? The Awaited One is tarrying, and the bodies of these mutes, of these immobile and speechless guests are being devoured. Humbly, in silence, Joana Carolina takes her place, her hands joined together, among Meadows, Wolfes and Burrs, among Lilies, Berries and Heathers, among Lambs, Quinceys and Amaryllis, among Roses, Lyons and Daisies, among Reeds, Crabbes and Veronicas, among Martens, Jasmines, Irises, Hollies, Dales, Violets, Maples, Foxes, Ivies, among Cranes, and Fishes, and Ferns, among Willows, and Hawks, and Fields, in the dress she wore on Sunday afternoons and enveloped by the silence that was her only companion.

Baroque Tale or Tripartite Unity

HER DRESS is old and sumptuous, velvet with a golden design on a crimson background, little rural and domestic scenes, a joyous, bustling, glimmering universe, wrapped around the black undulations of her body. The monkey, bound by a thin rusty chain which she holds in her hands, watches me attentively from under her left armpit, its leathery hands resting on the dancers who play tambourines and flutes and kick their feet in the air around a tree, and on the hunter shooting his crossbow at a pelican in flight.

—Do you know this man?

—What happens if I say I don't?

—I heard that you lived with him for some time. You even had a child.

—He never wanted to see the kid, that bastard. Not even once.

Coils of hair, eyes like almonds, round cheeks, flaring nostrils, arched lips, breasts like spiral shells. Behind her, on the wall, cages with birds, all in profile and silent, canaries, parakeets, scarlet with iridescent wings, white with blue tails, black with violet hues, green with white markings under their eyes, silver beaks, jasper breasts.

—How can I recognize him? He and his cousin are so much alike. And both are named José.

—His cousin's name is José Pascásio. His is José Gervásio. But now he's using another name.

—Why didn't he want to see the kid? Why didn't he marry you?

—Because I'm black. Good enough to lie with, but not to stand next to at the altar.

—Do you care if he dies?

—For me it would be a relief. I'd like to see him in a hole in the ground.

—Then you'll tell me where he lives.

Sharp and cunning the expression on her face. A small scar, parting her chin in the middle. I put the small roll of bills on the table. The monkey rushes over, grabs it, tries to bite into the money.

—Count it.

—I know how much it is. I have a good eye. I can count money from afar.

—Asking for more won't do you any good.

—Do you know how many men I have to go to bed with in this rotten town to make half that?

The monkey looking at me over her left shoulder; over the right one; over the table. The white hairs around its head, its mummy paws, its shiny and malicious little eyes. Its voice like sharp little bites. It leaps onto one of the cages and all the birds flutter around, frightened.

—Why don't you move?

—I want to live near you-know-who.

—He lives in town, then.

—No, but he comes every week. The place where he lives is worse than this.

—Where is it?

—I'll give you the information you want only if you tell me why you want to murder him.

—You mean execute him. I don't know why. I'm obeying orders.

—Take your money. He's coming tomorrow. If I make up my mind, I'll show you the prey.

I have conquered the steep hill of Congonhas, full of Christs and immobile apostles, of restless rams, of indifferent goats, I am standing in the church plaza, in the purple light of the setting sun, amidst the prophets and the few animals—the tame lion, the diminutive whale—staring at those heavy leaves of sandstone with Latin sentences, those hands, unarmed and powerful, those vacant eyes. The woman, now wearing a white dress, half hidden behind Nahum's cloak, is waiting for José Gervásio, who will arrive at the church shortly. Next to Baruch's sandals, my arms crossed, I observe the steep street from which my victim will come. I cannot hear a thing. In the silence, treason is brewing, a net woven by the black woman's hand. She will point him out to me: "This is the man." I will give her the reward, she will be able to move.

Or:

The funeral in the streets of Ouro Preto. Covered with purple ribbons, fluttering in the cold afternoon wind, the somber silverplated coffin, with its fuses, niellos, fretwork and hooks on the cobblestone street, amidst the closed doors, balconies, old roofs. Two long lines lead the procession, the men on the right (I among them), the women on the other side, some with lilies, others with roses, dahlias, immortelles. Further back, the lines are entirely made up of women. Ahead of the coffin, a brotherhood, I do not know which one: red surplices and tall candles; accompanying it, two pairs of children, with bouquets and wreaths: carnations, lilies, banderoles. A bald priest with a wrinkled face is praying, flanked by three young altar boys with scarlet tunicles and white lace chasubles; one of them is swinging the censer. Among the group closing behind the procession the black woman and I walk side by side, she in a cotton dress with green and blue waves overlapping. She forcefully takes the arm of a man, they look into each other's eyes. My hunt, my search of months, is finally over, I will be able to return to Pernambuco. I fix in my memory these features so long sought for, and which, as a result, had acquired the artificial life born of portraits. I would not have been able to discover them by myself. Bells are tolling. Great black peacocks fly over the funeral.

Or:

I am in Tiradentes, in the parish church, in the City Hall, on the street, at the fountain, a hat on my head. The church is full of ladders and scaffoldings, men are working to uncover the acanthus, the leaves, the foliage, palm leaf decorations and garlands hidden beneath the whitewash. Workmen talk, standing several feet from each other, about a priest who hated the town, so much that he threw salt on the images to ruin them. Out on the street, under the green cypresses, children are throwing stones at the birds. The clerks glide through the silent rooms of the City Hall, where pensive lions adorn the decrepit walls. Even the soldiers open and close the doors with circumspection, disappearing in the concave shadows, without arrogance. The chief of police looks at me and assents. Furtive old men in felt shoes skirt along the corridors. The mayor deposits the tax collection in the clay money box, a fierce and hairy fish with a coiling tail. With most of the houses closed up, almost all the dogs starved to death or left. You cannot hear any barking or roosters crowing. Standing erect at the windows, girls with wavy hair wait for the passage of death with somnambulant pupils. A man leans against the wall; indifferent to him, a gray bird describes a sinuous curve and enters a hole a foot and a half from his head, where it must have made its nest; the man ignores the bird as well. Sitting on a bench next to the fountain, the black woman tells me that every Thursday, with business as an excuse,

José Gervásio comes to see a woman at four, then goes back home on the eight o'clock train. But at times, when he can't come, he sends José Pascásio with some money. I ask her if lovers come to sit on these benches around the gargoyle on full moon nights. She answers that Tiradentes is a town where not even lovers exist. She seizes my arm and looks over my shoulder: "Here he comes. Don't forget his face." I pass her the money, caress the revolver in my pocket.

She is lying on the bed naked, with her knees drawn up and her legs spread apart, her left arm resting next to her hip, her right hand on the curved railing of the bed. The chintz bedspread with poppies, interlaced palm leaves and great magnolias hides her sex and covers her up to the right shoulder. With her round belly button and sloping shoulders, she reminds me of an angel raising a chalice I saw somewhere. On the dresser, in a lamp with a shade the color of mud held firmly in the claws of a small dragon, the light tarnishes her body with verdigris. Next to the lamp, a bluish plastic fruit dish imitating glass, with bananas, oranges and two lemons almost white, translucent as eggs. Above the dresser, several butterflies with spread wings and colored beetles, pinned and framed. The house is big, walls with decals of garlands, dentils, pale violets and faded rose apples, tile floor, little furniture. Smell of mildew. The black woman keeps talking about José Gervásio, savoring every word. Mice scurry in the dark, cockroaches flutter around. The light projects on the worm-eaten ceiling a muddy star, full of holes. The house is so empty, the town so quiet, that it sounds as if there were another woman talking in another room, with the same voice, dark and crossed by flying roaches, skeletal mice. She says what she is planning to do with the money she received for her information: buy perfumes, a gold wedding ring, a collection of butterflies, sunglasses, an anklet, a silver knife, printed velvet clothes. "Nothing for the kid?" "No." "Why?" "Because." "Where is he?" "You don't know me, and yet you ask about the kid. His father never did. He didn't even want to see him. He showed up when my belly was out to there, spoiling for a fight, he wanted me to leave. He was getting married, didn't want me around. I hit him on the head with a stool, opened a slit bigger than my own. I left my mark." "He was right about not wanting to see his son." Without hearing me (did I really say that aloud?) she goes on. Or rather: she goes back to the beginning, the middle, to the tortuous turns of her story, cursing men, a man, this Gervásio who is at the same time himself and me, and others, talks about her son and men in a cavernous voice. Her sex, covered with green hair thick and shiny like steel, is exposed now. With my forefinger, I slowly draw a spiral on her belly: "I, too, have a son I'm never going to see." "What if you knew he was dying?" "Even so, I wouldn't." "You're just like him, then. He didn't come, when the boy died." Naked, sitting on the bed, she shows me the picture of the dead child and his clothes, diapers, wool shirts, booties, toys, ribbons, some faded roses. "When did he die?" "Last week, in this bed. To-morrow I'm going to buy some hydrangeas, some lil-ies-of-the-valley, to take to the cemetery. That's another reason I don't want to leave this town." "So you had been here for some time, when you had the child." "I wanted to get even with his father. And now I have, I pointed him out with this hand. Why are you looking at me like that? Do you think I did wrong?" "I don't judge anyone. That's not my job. I simply bought some-thing I was interested in, something you had to sell." "You can't be what you say you are. Tell me if I was wrong." She has put the dead child's mementos back in the big dresser drawer. She is standing next to the bed, greenish in the light carefully held by the small dragon.

Then:

Reaching for my shirt, I begin to get dressed. The sheet of glass between us shatters into fragments we cannot see; this lukewarm, rusty, smooth and excitable sketch becomes threatening, vomits all over me her flagellated intimacy, demands that I judge her. And I will not even be able to lie with her again on this bed reeking of lavender and putrescent roses.

—Why are you leaving?

—Because now you exist. Unfortunately.

—What did I do wrong?

—You began to be. I can't explain. But a whore, a

victim, can't exist. If they do, they open a wound in the executioner. Do you understand?

—You can leave if you want. But don't give me that stuff.

—I'm leaving because I can't find any peace here anymore.

Or:

Faced with my silence, she can only think of one response: open again the drawer where she thinks she has preserved a past reduced to dust and throw it at me, try to infect me with her disease, drag me into that business between her life and a dead child, annihilate me. Threatened by the invasion of these vestiges, which the woman intuitively knows capable of worming their way into a stranger with the same voracity and the same power of multiplication of roaches and mice, I turned the lamp off, and finding the supple resistance of her body in the darkness I let myself fall with her on the bed, where the child had died and where his clothes, wilted roses and useless toys were scattered. In the darkness, the presence of these things—all without master, without use—was prevailing, trying to gnaw at me as if I could see them. The black woman, sinking her nails in my back and moaning as if that pressure hurt her, was still asking if she was wrong, if she had done wrong in betraying that man whose negligence perhaps had caused the death of the bastard on whose remains we were wrestling. I was describing my own act between my clenched teeth, my eyes closed in the darkness, struggling to destroy the words uttered and their corrupting meaning at the same time.

Or:

I place the tip of my tongue between my teeth, look into her eyes with such intensity that I pass through them and cease to see them. I know she is intent on luring me into the trap with which human beings, like spiders, capture those outside the web. Butterflies, faded rose apples, poppies, magnolias, violets and garlands close in around me. The woman is trying to suck me into her guilt and nostalgia, her rotting love, maybe. I hear her calling me a murderer. She is wrong, though. I am, at most, an executioner, in any case nothing more than an exemplary employee. In order to do my job well, I do not discuss orders, do not judge them, avoid weighing them in my hand, as well as weighing or judging my fellow men, I just obey them. It behooves the executioner, with his reticent ethics, to become immune to the cunning and even pernicious intrusion of that which is human. I must hold on to some neuter image, a cube for example, until this woman has exhausted herself with her attempts to involve me and I can—with the same disinterestedness—leave her forever or lie with her again and possess her, beat her perhaps, but without any anger.

Outside, among these old moonlit houses, through these winding streets, I remember my childhood. My sister, with her black braids and a glass compote dish full of red and yellow cashew fruits in her arms, is in the garden, hiding behind a black mouse. A white peacock with a golden and blood-red tail approaches and greedily devours the fruit as my sister watches, paralyzed, leaving only the empty compotier. The mouse turns around and swallows my sister up in the twinkling of an eye. He swears eternal love to the peacock, though, and leaves him alone. The capricious peacock spreads his tail, picks up a knife and bleeds the mouse, slitting his throat. My sister again, sitting on her little chair, her braids on her breast. A dog comes, takes her away and marries her. He makes a cake with dirt and decorates it with rubies and bones for my sister to eat. She refuses, my brother-in-law swallows up cake and dish. My sister returns to our house. We have breakfast together. I tear off a piece of bread and raise it to my mouth. My sister points to the loaf of bread in the middle of the table. *It's a little boy! Are you going to eat him?* I answer that it is not a boy, but a scorpion. Our dishes and cups are forever brimming with children, alligators, scorpions, buffaloes, horses, mothers and flowers, which we feast upon with a smile. Somewhere in a church a bell is pealing. I do not count the strokes and I do not have my watch with me. Empty streets. I do not know where the inn is, and there is nobody around to ask. The town, armillary sphere of silences, dissolving in the acid of the moon.

"Are you the man who's looking for my son?" "No."

"I'm his father." "That's what I figured." "I thought you'd be older." "Older than who?" "Than you." "No, I'm my age. Not a day older." "May I ask how old?" "Twenty-two. I'm neither looking for a son nor a father. I'm looking for a person, just him, and him alone, with no relation to anyone." "To kill him?" "That's none of your business. " "What do you mean, none of my business? I heard you wanted to kill my son." "I've already told you I don't."

From the back the man looks normal, with his suppliant air, his hunched back, one shoulder higher than the other; from the front, if you do not pay much attention, there's nothing special about him either. If you observe him more closely, though, you can see that his dark glasses, too big for his face maybe, have a strange purpose: that of concealing the absence of his left eye, which does not exist, never did, he does not have an eye socket or an eyebrow, the tissue behind the dark glass is reminiscent of those pictures of naked women whose pubis was touched up in the negatives, a camouflage more glaring than the frank reproduction of the model. To compensate for this, below the right eye, in its proper place, another right eye observes me, coldly, through the lens. The two eyes take turns, they do not blink at the same time. On the worn carpet, where three gazelles among embroideries, sedges and digitate leaves, can still be discerned, the character's feet, in a pair of heavy yellow shoes, go back and forth, as if they were studying a way of attacking me.

—My son's name is José Gervásio. I'm sure you came here after him, but I beg you by all you hold dear, go back to where you came from. Say you couldn't find him, or that he was already dead.

—A promise is a promise. Get out.

For the first time the two eyes have closed. The old man holds his hands out to me at the height of my stomach, his palms up, trembling:

—I came to offer myself in the place of my son. I'm begging you.

—I don't have any choice in the matter.

His hands remain fixed in a gesture of entreaty, so effective and easy. His voice, on the contrary, resembles the one that implored me about as much as an aluminum structure before and after a violent explosion in its foundation. The two right eyes pierce me, throwing me off balance.

—Then, since you won't do as I ask, I'll go to the police.

—It's no use. I *am* the police.

Or:

He does not hold his hand out to me. He remains standing in the threshold, sullen. I close the door. Bowing slightly, he gives me his hat, his umbrella, sits down and remains silent, sucking his teeth. He has a frightened and submissive look. His black shoes are so old they look gray. He cleans his glasses with the tip of his tie, with somber boughs and sanguine honeysuckle.

—My real name isn't José Gervásio.

—I know. It's Artur. It wasn't easy to find you.

—And now that you have found me...I'm not like the others. I don't run from my persecutors. I hear you're looking for me? Well, then: here I am.

—This is the first time. Until today you've been an escape artist.

—What do you want from me?

—You'll see.

—You want to kill me? Is that it? Of course it is. That's what I've been, all my life: the sacrificial lamb. The immolated one.

He shows me the picture, in a delicate frame with stars and imbrications. He in swimming trunks, long hair, a beard, his feet and wrists tied with rope, on a cross. His mother on her knees, her hands clasped together in supplication, her eyes heavenward. Further back, an old man with dark glasses. Then what we heard was true, that this man traveled around the interior of Bahia, in the area of the São Francisco river, with his father and mother, carrying on the back of a mule the cross on which he had them crucify him. He put a leather bag at the foot of the cross, people came, gave alms, prayed. His parents exploited him, traveled by train or bus while he went on foot with the mule and the cross.

—I'm going to tell you something horrible, which hurts to this day. Have you ever heard of Santo Sé? It's not far from Juazeiro. I had been on that cross for over twenty-four hours, almost without eating anything. There were towns where what they gave me wasn't even enough to feed the mule. But in Santo Sé it was glorious. Like this…(He points to the walls of the room, where the painted border, now in a state of decay, once depicted pineapples, bows and pink mangoes). A horn of plenty. There were even some big bills in the bag. Well, when night fell and the people went to sleep, my father and mother ran away with the money. I was crying from the cross, begging them for God's sake not to leave me. *Father, mother, why have you forsaken me?* They ran off on the mule without even looking back. No sacrifice surprises me.

—You seem to be grateful to your old folks.

—I'm not grateful. I've forgiven them, as I forgive everything. As everybody should. And, at the same time, I'm taking my revenge. I go everywhere in my carriage, while they walk. What do you want from me?

—You said it yourself, a while ago. I want to kill you.

He was cleaning his glasses again. He stops and looks at me puzzled, as if I had already shot him or pulled my knife. "I haven't done you any harm." "No, you haven't." "So?! What's my crime?" "I don't know." "Why must I die?" "I don't know and I don't care."

—You don't know how…to forgive.

—Forgive?…I'm a loyal agent and I intend to kill you one of these nights, when you return from your daily visit to your mother.

—I can go to the police.

—You won't. You've been running from the Law for years.

Having said this, we remain silent for the indispensable interval between what has been said and the sentence he finally ventures, in the way of a threat, hesitating over each syllable:

—What if I kill you first?

—That would be one of the only two ways of surviving.

—What's the other?

I write on a piece of paper, in numbers big enough for him to read even without glasses, the amount, exactly the same, paid to the black woman the day before yesterday to point him out to me. He put all the money he had in his pockets on the table, along with a ring. I gave him the ring back, kept the rest.

—Tell the desk clerk to send up the bill. I'm leaving.

From the window, I see him getting into the carriage, a fragile spider, iron wheels, pulled by a melancholy sorrel with flop ears. He whips the horse and leaves, without looking up.

Or:

I was not expecting a visit from the black woman. I do not recall giving her any information as to where I would stay, I do not think I told her my name, either, yet I find it perfectly natural for her to be here, with new shoes, clothes and purse, exuding a perfume she must have poured over herself without parsimony, *Fleur de Rocaille* maybe, and which must not be very common in this musty room. The dress (sunflowers on an ultramarine blue background) goes well with the serge of the sofa, the color of corn, with a worn tapestry of garlands, scepters and fleur-de-lis. I know from the very first moment that she regrets having come and is debating whether she should tell me what brought her here. While she is deliberating, she imitates with visible effort the conversation and behavior of a regular visitor, criticizing, for example, the separation of the sexes still in force in certain places of worship in Minas, or asking about countries where, according to what she was told, blacks are not considered human beings, compelling me to express my opinion, which I summarize thus: "Every country has its customs. It's not for us to judge them." She mentions with a smile the flowers she put on her son's grave and two pieces of printed silk she bought yesterday, one with birds, another with leaves. While she talks, she finally makes up her mind and confesses what I already suspected. She told José Gervásio about me, thus sinking deeper and deeper into an impossible game of betrayals and confessions of disloyalty, which are in turn new treacheries subsequently divulged. I listen to her without moving, remembering the glaucus undulations of her body, certain she will ask me if she did wrong, if what she did can be forgiven, as if these queries and the answers they elicit could alter the nature and the consequences of her actions.

—Nothing kept you from talking to José Gervásio. It was` my mistake not to demand your silence in our agreement. Did he reward you in any way for the information?

—He said that he already knew and that it didn't matter. How could he know?

—I'm going to pay you the same amount I gave you before. Go back and tell him that I left today. That you managed to convince me. But now your loyalty is part of the deal. I'm only asking you to keep the secret for two days. Tomorrow, when he comes back from the visit to the woman he calls his mother, I'll execute him. Two days only. It's not much. I'll give you half the money now and the other half later.

Before the dream, or before the part I remembered clearly, there was a monotonous and rather long part in which my servile nature and my master's tyranny became evident. Starting from the moment he orders me to go to the village, to see someone or bring some message to an even more powerful lord, the incidents become connected to one another and gain strength. In a black carriage, pulled by two horses, I turned around in the courtyard paved with flagstone, scattering hens, pigs, ducks and turkeys. I was holding my hat in my hands and receiving the orders, my eyes lowered. I have barely given the signal of departure, with a loud whiplash, when I hear my master's voice, imperious, calling after me. The noise of the carriage and of the horses allows me to turn a deaf ear to him with no fear of punishment. So I crack the whip with assurance, swearing through my teeth, overcome by an anger that throws me into a paroxysm. The desperate voice calls me again. Letting the wind carry it away, I yell at the horses and, drunk with anger, race along the road which I know as well as my pockets. I can feel my master following close on my heels. I act as if I did not know he was pursuing me, I begin to sing, still shouting and whipping the horses hard: they go faster, stretching out their necks. Cats, dogs, rabbits and sheep get squashed between the wheels of the carriage, the wind has blown my hat away. The mouth of the tunnel through which we both will have to pass is opening ahead of us. I put the handle of the whip between my teeth and pull up on the reins deliberately, to slow the gallop and allow the master to catch up with me…In complete darkness, the two carriages continued at full speed, one next to the other, without giving ground. The horses' hooves were pounding, neither of us was saying a word, the smell of leather and sweat was suffocating me. In spite of the darkness, I could see the walls of the tunnel, painted red: oxen and panthers, falcons, serpents and jackasses, pelicans, peacocks, does, dragons, turtles, lions and elephants, all flying past me like bats. Suddenly, I thought: "Now!" and drove my carriage against the master's, pushing it against the blood-red animals of the tunnel, while I lashed about with my whip shouting like a madman: "Take this, and this, and this!" The master was cursing in a muffled voice. I grabbed him, felt the roughness of his neck between my fingers, his blood throbbing, his strangled cry. "Take this!" I pushed him from the carriage. As he

was falling he gave off a smell of burnt hair. I wel-
comed with ferocious joy the cry of agony beneath the
wheels and the flying hooves, made my whip whistle
through the air. The horses were spurred on more by
my laughter and a cloud of flies than by the whip. I
enter the house I was sent to. Almost at the same instant, very pale, my master arrives and says to me: "Some
servant we've got!" I ask him, humbly as usual: "What
have I done?" The host, hearing me, intervenes: "Your
master is just giving you a hard time. I can tell from
your voice that you haven't done anything. Go on, sit
there." I sat down, opened a book and eagerly began
to discourse on the arabesques, festoons, borders,
conches and scrollwork that illustrated it. I declared
myself inferior to all enigmas and apologized for having the gift of penetrating them.

Thick clouds covering the moon. I listen to the silence, which will soon be broken by my shots. I picture it: large glass bowl, nocturnal mold of the winding streets, of the hills, of the empty churches, of the
houses with jutting eaves. Bodies safely tucked under
blankets. The bedbugs arrive with circumspection, steal
into the beds, vie with the mosquitoes for human blood;
on the ceilings and in the window frames, under the
furniture, spiders spit out their threads; termites drill
holes in the wood, weevils hollow out grain in the
warehouses, beetles dizzily drone hitting against walls,
moths flutter around the lamps, scorpions, ants, centi-

pedes, crickets and roaches are swarming all over the ground, grasshoppers are eating the leaves of the trees, ticks and flies sting the skin of horses, goats and cattle. I concentrate on the weight of the revolver on my ileum. Everything must be fast and neutral, so that the act to be performed does not lose its impersonal character. The execution must be like affixing a seal to a text to be signed. A little earlier than I expected (I did not hear the bells striking ten thirty) I hear, still far off, the hooves and the clatter of the wheels on the stones, disturbing the frogs and toads that leap across the street. Mentally, I measure the space between myself and the noise, finding a certain beauty in this convergence, in this man approaching his executioner with such precision and certainty. Bullet in the chamber, I calculate the distance: the shots must be fired without any possibility of error and, at the same time, the victim must not see me beforehand. He might lay the whip to the horse and dodge the bullets. The spider is in the street. Under the little canvas top, within my gun's sights, a figure holds the reins. It stops, strikes a match. I aim at its head, thinking my mission has been accomplished: the match goes out, the figure bends over, falls slowly, its legs get caught in the step of the carriage. The horse remains immobile, all the insects indifferent, not a door opens, not a window. I see that I have killed the black woman, always undecided in her choices, a victim of the lack of definition that was a fault in itself and led me into error as well.

Or:

Stars and moon illuminate the knife blade. In the silence I hear the joints of the town creaking and decay creeping over the two-hundred-year-old walls, over the beams and the girders, over the colors of the saints and their bodies, over the choirs, the carvings, gildings, altars and moldings, over the windows, the ceilings, the chairs, the beds, the drawers, the crosses, the oratories, decay with its fungi, its insects, its sharp claws, its corrosive tongue. Everything, suddenly, looks like a knife blade to me: the letter and the inkblot, the bird and the shot, intimacy and distance, building, destroying, being born, living, dying. I hide the blade in its sheath. Facing myself, less than six feet away, I ask: "Am I sure?" I answer: "Am I?" Before it occurs to us who is to make inquiries and who is to solve them, we hear the trot of a horse, the light wheels of a spider turning on the pavement, while the church bells strike once and we both move away, I on the right hand side of the street, I on the left, I hesitant, I determined, waiting for the condemned. The black horse—which appears white in the moonlight—comes, pulling the spider with its master inside. Hiding in the shadows, I remain still, watching the animal, the carriage and the man; but I move forward, and before the whipped horse has a chance to gallop away, I jump into the spider and do my duty. From the street, the now useless weapon in my hand, I see the sad vehicle moving away, hear a stifled cry amidst the noise of the wheels and of the hooves, I see myself jump off, jump off and come back to me, while the spider races through the streets, with its wounded passenger.

Or:

I do not know why this hirsute dog, with huge paws, so similar to the lion curling at Daniel's feet, is following me. It was waiting for me on the way out and walked on ahead of me, I ahead of it, down the empty moonlit streets. Why do I think of my sister and her black braids on full moon nights? The Monkey was climbing a banana tree, with the heavy basket of jaboticaba and pitomba berries and sapodillas, which he was eating. My sister hit him with a stick. The Monkey ran away and still managed to eat a passion fruit, currants, a cherimoya, Brazil cherries, mangoes, inga fruits, sugarapples, guavas. The Ant came and ate the Monkey. The Hare came and ate the Monkey again. Then my sister and I went out arm in arm with him, we climbed up into a jackfruit tree, were surrounded by white dogs. Now I see dogs in the stars. Skeletons of dogs, dog ears, dog skin cut open, bitches and puppies, dog mandibles, winged dogs, with wavy manes, wagging tails, horns and crowns. They gallop on their big paws, like this dog's, they bark, and even the skins without dog, the bones without skin run high above, the entire town vibrates with the galloping. In the absolute silence, I hear the horse's unhurried steps, the iron wheels, the steps of the horse. The dog moves away, heads for the spider. It has stopped at the beginning of the street, someone has gotten off and is coming toward me. I take out the revolver, aim at the heart. *Do not allow any dialogue. Eliminate the victim quickly. Do not allow him, under any circumstances, to breach the distance that protects me from his wiles.* I lower the weapon: he is not the person I am looking for.

—I came in his place. Let me die in my son's place.

The dog, sitting, looks at me. The horse gets tired of waiting, comes pulling the spider along, stops next to us. The old man thinks that he will draw me into some troubled and difficult game, full of questions, of pressure, of deliberations, that he will introduce uncertainty, the vacuum and imbalance in my limpid rigor. Without answering, I fire my gun, blow his brains out. The horse bolts away, dragging the old carriage, the dog starts to bark. In the moonlight, I examine the old man lying on the sidewalk: he now seems to be looking at me with three eyes. The dog sniffs him.

Pastoral

WITHOUT those thick glasses, my dead godfather looks like another man. He is another man. He was looking at me from behind his lenses, saying all those things about my mother, the day he gave me Canária. The sermon breathed offense and cruelty, it came from his nostrils; he did not walk fast either, but with cautious little steps, the steps of a turtle. Since he was dead, and I was his godson, my father could not do anything but take me to town with him. There he is, sitting with his mouth open, listening to the many bells of Goiana tolling for his friend. When he is distracted his mouth hangs open; his eyes never rest, though, they scrutinize everything with diffidence. Even when he is not talking, his voice resonates in my ears. I hear his voice day and night, ceaselessly. It is not for him, or for my godfather, it is for the six women from Goiana, strange animals the like of which I have never seen at the farm (two sitting on the bench, their faces resting on their hands, the third one standing, in the sun, tying her hair up, another staring into space, sitting on the sofa by herself with her arms resting on the back, and two plucking petals from carnations and scattering them on the corpse), it is for them that I would like to have six eyes. Aliçona, is she a woman? She wears a dress, sure, similar to these girls' skirts and blouses. But is she a woman? When she bathes in the river, naked, she looks like a gnarled trunk, gray and green, thick, covered with slime. Her hair is black. Even so, I see in her verdigris face, wide and creased by lines, ages that fill me with fear. These girls' are not frightening. Delicate skin, soft hands, white or print dresses, earrings, light shoes. How pretty they are! They could play with me, perhaps, roll in the leaves, sleep in my bed. This, which sounds like a chorus of cicadas, is the perfume of my six Goianians.

No one can see me here. Canária meekly yields to my caresses. With my eyes closed, I try to bite the blaze on her forehead. Thinking about the girls' perfume, I drown myself in her young mare's smell, still hot from the sun. The light becomes entangled in the branches, pleasure mounts, slowly creeping up my legs. My body transcends its limits, merges with the shiny golden flanks, with the arch of the back, the raised head. The sun disappears earlier on these plains. The spongy light reflected by the clouds filters through the branches of the old orange trees beneath which the mare and I are hiding. Night has fallen and soon the first stars will appear through the leaves. Because of this, and also because of my long hair, which covers my ears (months pass before someone remembers to cut it), I cannot see my profile. Joaquim, far away, is felling a tree; I feel the ax blows, muffled, in my knees. One more day for Canária to mature, one more day before we take her to the horse waiting for her in some pasture, horse of cacti, mane of agave, tail of burrs.

Our father, with his dead left arm, yells out Balduíno's name and orders him to cut my hair. "He looks like a Veronica!" Everything that reminds him of a woman fills him with anger. "Shave it off!" Balduíno Gaudério is the youngest son of my father's first wife, who died after twenty years of marriage. "I never heard that woman raise her voice, Baltazar. Why say anything? My father only asked that she be faithful and do her share of the work. But when she died she let out a scream, an *amen* to make anyone's hair stand on end. Her life left her with that cry." My father does not understand why Balduíno Gaudério never grew up; he can only find one reason: he was bewitched, someone gave him the evil eye when he was a child. There seems to be, in Gaudério, a man made for a body bigger than his own: he weighs almost as much as Domingos or Jerônimo. He is not as coarse as our two brothers and seems to feel some friendship for me, even though he does not show it, to avoid reproaches. He takes the blade sharpened by Joaquim and shaves my head, without saying a word. I do not speak either. Standing with my arms hanging at my sides, submissive, I stretch out on the ground, follow the operation and even take pleasure in it. It is so rare to feel someone's touch, even a rough one. Not even Aliçona, who is a woman, caresses me. Aliçona is a woman, Baltazar? Yes. No, she is not. She goes around the big house sullenly, with the air of someone condemned to carry its entire weight on her shoulders. She sweeps the broom across the tiles perfunctorily, sweeps like a blindman, dusts carelessly, washes the dishes and our clothes in almost no water. Barefoot, the skin on her heels cracked, her toenails horny and yellow, always whispering and laughing to herself, full of hatred. No, she is not a woman. From behind Balduíno, I look at my neck, at my pale nape. I never understood why I am made of woven vines. And how old am I? I have no idea. Balduíno, our brothers Jerônimo and Domingos, my father and Joaquim, the distant relative who got off his horse nearly eight years ago and made himself at home here, have also forgotten. They do not know whether they should treat me like a man or like a boy. They all agree, though, that I bear a strong resemblance (they never say to whom), that I am always going to be a dead weight and that one day, even though I do not mean to, I will betray them. It is possible. I am indolent and I lack muscle.

The copper lamp lit on the milkwood table hewn by adz on which we eat. When we hunch over the blue enameled tin dishes, we always look as if we were crying: the table is low, almost as low as a bed. Our father sits at one end, opposite Joaquim. He is the tallest and the whitest of us all. Almost completely black hair, falling on his forehead. The paralyzed left arm has not diminished his energy. At his right sit Jerônimo and Domingos, both nearing forty and still single; at his left, in charge of cutting the old man's meat, when necessary, Balduíno. My father's head is turned towards me. He is looking at me, an amused, sideways look. All his looks, even when he is angry, seem amused. Joaquim, his hand stretched toward the water jug, is also looking at me. Face the color of earth, bald head, bushy eyebrows and hairy ears. His skull shines under the lamplight. Domingos mumbles, laughs for no reason. He brings the knife to his mouth, with a big piece of sun-dried meat on its tip. Jerônimo, forgetting the silverware, has raised both hands and is droning his usual accusations against me. He has a sour look: I taste lemon on my tongue when he looks at me. Balduíno and I keep our heads down, hunching over the blue dishes. The shadows of those at the sides of the table are larger than father's and Joaquim's, who are sitting farther away from the lamp. The shadow of Jerônimo's hands on the blackened tiles across which bold white-bellied possums sometimes scurry, is almost invisible. I place my hands on my shoulders and sadly kiss my shaved head.

I watch myself sleeping, my limbs spread apart, five-pointed star. At the same time I hear the mare's bells in the stable and the sound of her hooves trotting in my dream. I occupy this huge room, which used to be my parents', all by myself. There are no longer any images in the black oratory; harnesses hang from the inch thick nail stuck in the wall from which my mother used to suspend the purse with her jewels at night; the locked chest, which is never opened—its four keys must have gotten lost—and where perhaps shoes and clothes are molding, is still there; in the wooden box, painted red and blue, I keep horns, stones, bones of animals, cowbells and the few coins Gaudério occasionally gives me. After his first wife died, my father did not change anything for his second marriage. We were all born on this iron bed with the metal frame. And there, on the mattress of wormwood and damp straw, grow, night after night, the vines I am made of, they grow quickly, but not as fast as Canária.

Naked, my legs in the murky water, half a gourd in my hand, I climb out of the rain water ditch, pulling my mare by the rope. The color of my skin tends to bay; compared to the copper-colored mare, it is as white as the moon. They like to torment me, Canária. Even yesterday, at supper, what did they do? I am a good-for-nothing, worth less than a dog, because I cannot even bark. And I am cruel. Jerônimo claims that he knows things, when a horse is not good to mount; when a dog will attack people; in me, he sees cruelty: I am the sudden drop, in a river that can be waded. The hidden whirlpool. Domingos was laughing, grinding me between his dirty teeth. Father was giving me looks harsher than Jerônimo's words, even though amused. For Joaquim I am a poisoned fish. If I could, Canária, I would drown them one by one, even Balduíno, who did not take my side. They talked about the woman. Not about her name; not about what she did. They talked without talking. Don't they recognize an animal by its tracks? I am the tracks of a stolen animal. Or of a fugitive one. My mouth pressed against the mare's forehead, against her damp blaze, I see the midday sun above the valleys, the mountains, like a herd of a hundred white goats, all with bells strung around their horns. My body is made of the same malleable and tough fiber out of which horses are molded.

Until today, only my godfather talked to me the way you talk to a human being. I brought you this mare, Baltazar, to keep you company. I know what it's like to live alone, like you. I, too, went through hell, believe me. And nobody knows. He is sitting in the shade of this tree, perched on its roots, sucking star fruits, his eyes like slugs glued to his glasses. A drawling and twangy voice, full of bad scratches. I like the little beast and choose for her, right then and there, the name Canária, Aliçona's sheep and Gaudério's goats suddenly do not mean anything to me anymore. None of these animals, whose docility I take for granted and whose rebellions enrage me, will ever have for me the beauty and the worth of Canária. I wonder how you came to be, Baltazar. How your mother could do such a thing, agree to marry that animal, while I was still alive. And have a son from him. Imagine, your father plowing that sweetness. People do such things! And the worst is that you look just like her. You can't remember, but seeing you is like seeing her. Ah, if only I had known. And I could have guessed. But I didn't have the courage, I always lived in fear. What did it matter if I was her son's godfather? I wonder where she is now! That bum was not the man for her. He liked gold, too much. That's what he saw: her gold. As for me, I would have taken her without all those jewels, those rings, those necklaces. Like a glass of water.

I do not say anything, but I understand. His words stay with me: the point of a knife sharpened by Joaquim could not carve them more deeply in wood. Did I know this black figure, standing on the porch, a huge cross of gold and diamonds, hanging by a heavy chain on her breast? No. Did I know those black leather shoes, those black cotton stockings, those long sleeves? No. And yet I see. She put a black silk veil over her head. Her face floats in the light of the stars, barely twinkling in the calm November night. It is, after all the decisions have been made, the last moment of hesitation. After all the ties have been cut, there was still this one hanging loose—and offering resistance. The house is quiet, the dawn, still distant, is beginning to form within the night. The roosters are sleeping. Not very far, a white horse, harnessed, is waiting for her. The metal of the stirrups, the buckles of the leather straps and the rivets adorning the harness do not shine as much as its white mane. Firefly horse. The man in the saddle, waiting for that pale woman, whose age is more or less that of her stepsons Jerônimo and Domingos, and who accentuates her paleness with her black blouses, with her loose sleeves, her black earrings, her two black braids tied with big black ribbons. Always covered with rings, some times four on the same finger, bracelets, gold chains around her neck. Her life absorbs its only nourishment from all these jewels; or maybe gold and stones drain her strength, suck her bones, drink her clear blood. The man, already in the saddle, gives just one order. To take, of all her treasures, only those she has had since she was a girl. No clothes. No shoes. Nothing my father gave her. Just your body and what you're wearing. The child isn't coming either.

The sun sets, red mouth and darting eyes. It falls, yellow, hard in its pride, amidst blood-red panaches. The bay mare, with me on her back, darts across the afternoon, four hooves in the wind, her tail prolonging the line of her back and her mane flying higher than her ears, as if forever launched in a gallop that reverberates in the distance. How she grew, in just a little over a year! I want to be like this, have this strength, gallop over my brothers, over Joaquim and his earth-colored face, over my father and his authority, go out in the world in search of my mother, kneel at her feet. The purples, the golds and the greens of the clouds blend with one another, three black vultures glide over the farm. On the ground, under the trees, I see the roots, their black claws. The strength of the body under mine, stretching into space, fast, in the sun, enters me and churns in my blood. I turn into twenty, a hundred pinwheels, green, purple, golden like the clouds, turning on top of the flying mare.

Of all the rooms, only one has a window: big, with thick panes, double hinges, iron handles. Under the weight of my body the bed sags, almost like a hammock. In the open window, I see moon, stars, countryside and stables, the movements of the older mares, Canária's flanks, the tinkling of her bell, smell of grass, of stale piss, the stallion in the smaller stable. I see everything. Won't someone give me half of a horse's body? Or half of Joaquim's body. He sleeps with a knife across his chest, his trunk is almost as wide as the table, he fills the end opposite my father's completely. If he were not so strong he would be a field hand, who takes orders and ordinary wages; instead he rules, makes decisions. It was he who brought the white-footed horse for Canária. Haughty head, wary look, clipped mane: in the stable, solitary, sun rays in his bones and blood, he waits for the morning. They will let my beasty loose in the courtyard, and then they will wait. With his mere presence, he will conquer her, he will be a more secure prison than the highest fence. Here she is circling around his chest, his mane, his hooves, without being able to escape. He neighs, kicks his front legs in the air, tears up the mare's entrails, with furor and glory.

I feel the weight of the scythe in my hand. I lit the tinplate lamp, to better judge the vigor and fire of the horse. On his legs, on his flanks and near his nostrils, the smoky light reveals the design of his veins. His dark hair, in the curves of his body, reflects the flame. He is a horse of iron, covered with rust. First, turning his head, he examined me with his left eye, enlarged with excitement and unbearably shiny. Then, reassured, he went back to his fresh hay. This body conceals in its belly the instrument of my humiliation. I test the edge of the scythe with my thumb. Nobody like Joaquim to sharpen steel, he could turn a knife's handle into a razor. I leaned over and stroke the horse between his legs. Little by little he begins to show his attributes, it is as if he were opening his breast and exposing, defenselessly, the source of life, then I close my eyes, set my jaw and, with my entire hand, my vine-woven arms tenser than ever, I seize the streaked penis and cut it off with the scythe, in a single short blow. The lord of mares and father of a hundred other horses, who was a sun in the pastures, comes apart in gushing blood, his quarters harnessed, as if succumbing to the weight of a carriage, he who never knew the yoke in his life. The shiny black eyes turn dim, a gray film covers them, his head struggles to stay up, the way it used to, in the fields where for years he unfurled his strength like a red banner, but soon it collapses on the ground, lifeless and dishonored. The light of the lamp flickers, the lustrous reflections on the horse's skin die out, the veins disappear, his quivering hooves turn whiter. The foaming blood is black and sweet-smelling.

Lying in the shade of a breadfruit tree, my back

covered with whip marks, the welts throbbing, I discover a red and unbalanced world. There is a tree of
delicate leaves, which stands out among the others:
vigorous, with a gnarled trunk and dense foliage. All
green, transparent green, thick green, heavy green, pure,
impure, green. The sky is red, red the ground. The
tinamous are singing. Gaudério's whipping was the
lightest–and the one that hurt most. The last one to
whip me. Even Joaquim put in his share, four firm lash-
ings, one after the other, the last time he pretended to
miss the target and hit my neck. After that, I did not
have the strength to cry out. The welts glisten, I look
at them over my shoulder: mimosa embers. If only the
girls who were keeping vigil over my godfather flew
over my back now, with their green cicada song!

On Canária's back, on top of the mountain, I see a
stretch of the creek, down below, where ducks are
swimming and a calf lies, chewing its cud, growing in
the morning. It was there. Some dresses were drying,
among men's shirts and the patchwork quilt. Aliçona is
time in human form, a growling time; and her black
clothes, nobody can say that they belong to a woman.
That is why she enters our house, sets the table, does
the wash, roasts the sun-dried meat, makes the mush.
Because she is not a woman. Those, though, were pretty
dresses, very different from Aliçona's clothes. One with
big red flowers, another the color of honey, a girl's
white dress, all on the line, billowing. It looked like a
conversation among dresses. I do not know the people

of this farm. The washerwoman, the owners of the dresses and the masters of the owners of the dresses, are they souls? Or perhaps only clothes live here? The one with the big flowers was dancing, telling some funny story, the honey-colored one was smiling. The men's clothes could not hear or see anything, but the white dress was calling me. There they are, more than the last time, all immobile, hanging on the line, spread on the stones on the banks of the creek and on the branches of two gooseberry bushes. I recognize the white dress among the branches.

In the cornfield, among the tall stalks and the swollen ears. In two, three weeks, they will be snapped from their stems by the hands of Jerônimo, Joaquim, Domingos, Balduíno Gaudério. My father, with the gestures of a master, will pull some off. The cornfield, luminous refuge. On one side, the crescent moon is rising, almost full. The sun has not set yet: it is sinking on the other side, face without ears, conniving eyes and a big fiery mouth. Naked, stretched out on the mare's back, her curly mane on my neck, in my hands the dress still damp, inhaling at the same time Canária's smell and the smell of soap, of corn and earth, I sob. The mare's back is hot, rough and slippery, the cloth of the dress frays between my fingers, a cicada is singing, the girl of the sofa is caressing my feet, my buttocks, my stiffened back, I see the sun and the moon, their two lights meet in my breast, I split in two, discover why I am crying, it is the silence, the pinwheels of pleasure are turning inside me, I forget everything, fall face down. Still sobbing. My face buried in the dress. Along the paths of my blood I hear the voice, a happy song, it is a man singing, and this man is walking toward me, impossible, because the man is myself in the prime of life. Canária is smelling the ground near the small of my back.

The moonlight, through the windowpanes, shines on the dress, lying on the floor, free again and even whiter than before. I am sitting on the bed, and standing by the oratory. From the stable comes the tinkling of Canária's bell, as clear as the dress. From the dinner table, thundering, come Joaquim's voice and Domingos' coarse laugh. Balduíno, small, always at our father's left, pretends to be smiling; for him, who has a small mouth, it is easy. Domingos is really laughing, he got up and is looking down, his vile hands open, wide apart. Jerônimo looks him over, with his sour eyes. My father, tall and white, his dead arm lying on the table, like a rag, blows his nose and stares at the wall, beyond the commotion and laughter. They are talking about Canária, the dead horse, what they will do tomorrow. Yearning to go to the corral, kiss Canária's dark flanks, chew her mane. I will not go. Canária is a possession I can no longer claim. Her master is the horse, a half-hour walk from here, which my father and brothers are talking about.

Lying on the wooden floor on top of the dress, I fell asleep, naked in the moonlight. Around me, the horns, the round stones, the coins, the cowbells without clappers, the animal bones, the shadows of the room, the harnesses on the nail, the empty oratory, the calm of the night. My brothers, my father, Joaquim, they too are drinking in their sleep the strength with which they will accomplish their tasks tomorrow. Which will take Canária? Jerônimo? Domingos? Will all of them go? I picture the horse: immobile, tall, a mountain, fiery eyes, huge chest, his tail like a black thick whirlwind. Galloping horses invade the room, bay, white, black, all covered with blood, all neighing, pursued by fierce hawks. The big horse does not budge.

I walk between the coolness of the night and the heat of the morning. I have not eaten: I was in a hurry, my stomach knotted up. What time did Jerônimo and Domingos leave? Will I run into them on the road? Below these valleys, these mountains, these plantations, there are rivers of fire, into which the sun plunges and the clouds of the East bathe every night. That is why they take on this color, red. The red dyes the green of the foliage, between blue and purple at this hour. The cattle scattered in the field are red as embers, and the goats, transfixed by the light, glass. The roosters' crow is red too. I do not know why I am going; I would rather not go, or never arrive. A wind is pushing me on, blowing over my shoulder, strong hot wind. I put a hobble on my ankles—but, even without wanting to, I go faster, lighter and lighter, step, half-step, trot, wind on my breast, morning taste. My green mane grows, my blue tail, and I gallop full of hatred, flying down this hill, I am a white horse, impetuous, hooves of stone, sharp teeth. Galloping, I raise my head above the crimson pastures, above the trees, the mountains and the birds flying, above the clouds of fire, the rising sun, and I neigh with all my might.

I see, in the eight men whose shadows are growing longer, tangled up with the shadow of the fence and of the horses, expressions of envy. Their eyes are fixed on the center of the corral, like people appraising someone else's wealth. One, very young, his black hair falling on his forehead, cannot conceal his pride behind his gaping mouth and drooping eyelids. He must be the master of the horse. Who is the center of everything. A beautiful animal, and of a very unusual color. Black, white tail and mane, shiny like corn silk when the corn is still green, and long, the way I would like mine to be. He gently bites Canária's left ear. The ground is trampled, turned over, full of hoof marks. They have been circling around the same spot for a long time, restless, the male around the female, the female around the male, as if tied to a post, but avoiding each other. Maybe they fought. Now, both immobile, the horse bites Canária's ear. Between the posts and the figures of the men leaning on the fence, none of whom noticed my presence, she must see me, unless she is blind. Will she break free from the horse's dominion, jump over the fence, come to me? She stands stiff, her hind legs spread apart. The skin on her flanks quivers. The men, always loud in these occasions, are not saying a word. Far off, in the calm of the morning, a lost sheep is bleating incessantly. The woman in black appears suddenly, on the other side of the fence, and urges me: "Go, Baltazar. It's worth it." I pick up a stone from the ground. Muffled ax blows in my knees. A cloud has passed, the sun is out again, and floods the animals with its light, an unexpected breeze ruffles the horse's mane. The cicadas' cries explode in the trees.

My slender body, woven with vines, but solid in appearance, becomes frail, a piece of clay, about to shatter under the horse's hooves. The eight men, out of surprise, and fear, keep from intervening. Less than sorrow, their faces express anger and incredulity, Canária has moved away, her head high and her ears raised. For me, this brief instant is a lightning bolt passing through my entire body. I still managed to throw my stone, without clear aim, at random. The horse's teeth, his galloping hooves fall upon me like thunder, and the white mane—cloud—blazes in the sun.

Lying on the table, without candles, with my hands crossed, the fox skin covering my groin. Silently sitting in the same place as always, my father, Joaquim and my brothers surround me. Thinking that they would have supper earlier (the cemetery is far), Aliçona has set the table: the blue dishes, the copper lamp. The few men who have come to my funeral are talking outside, they do not have the courage to come in. Some look up at the sky apprehensively. It is a cloudy, cold afternoon. It is going to rain before night. Perhaps with remorse, or with relief, maybe, since he will never again see this son of his, who does not resemble him at all, and who, every day, reminded him of the woman who dared to leave him, my father looks at me; the others keep their heads down. From the stable comes the sound of Canária's bell, still untouched by a horse. Now that I am naked and exposed, without the permanent and morose scowl with which I protected myself, I see what a child I was. Protruding nipples, a girl's shoulders. Jerônimo and Domingos brought me back lying across Canária's back. It was Balduíno Gaudério who washed my body and gently wiped off the dried blood. It was he who put the fox skin around my groin, him who crossed my hands and put a corn tassel between my fingers. He will not have to cut my hair at my father's command, never again. Of all of them, he is the only one who is crying, silent tears, almost without sobs. He envies me, the only one in this cold household who was capable of loving and of dying for it. His hands under the table, he promises to himself that he will have a wife, that he will love her, that he will never be like these other men.

Engagement

I♉ A L O N E in this room with green walls, one window shut, another open onto the night and the rhythmic sound of the waves, in the center of the irregular triangle at whose vertices are the Seminary, Abolition Square and the Convent of the Franciscans. We can see the city as if we were standing on top of the roof. The moonlight floods the sea and the streets, façades covered with tiles gleam in the silence. This will be the last of the numerous and pointless conversations we have had. The lighthouse is pulsating.

I One, serene, and master, after thirty years of office work, of my fate, should I relinquish this control now, by making a commitment to someone? I have torn myself loose from everything that hampered me, there are no more fractures in me, I will not see my colleagues again. I will now live my life with the inventiveness of an engineer who drives his locomotive off the tracks. No more beaten paths: improvisation is the rule.

—Only one thing worries me: I can't stop thinking about the problem of the windows at the Ministry.

♉ Torn between hope and fear, I have finally made up my mind. Two words have ruined my life: "tomorrow" and "later." Yes, this is the last time we will talk, I cannot stand his delays anymore. As for the trousseau, it will remain in the suitcases, in the drawers, until I die. How can I regret it, if my youth was even more useless to me?

—I don't know if I've already told you about the glass panes. Many were broken and most had humidity stains. Some were round, some oblong or starshaped. Some were quite large, nearly eighteen inches. Few windows remained intact. Then the boss put me in charge of studying the problem and making the necessary provisions. A ploy to keep me there: I was only a few months away from retirement.

—Why would he do such a thing?

—He's had this job for over thirty-nine years and hates to see people retire when it's time. He's waiting for compulsory retirement. Every employee who stays represents for him an endorsement of his love for reports and time sheets. I didn't give him this pleasure. At exactly the same moment I received the Official Gazette, I was writing this word: *sixty*. It's also my age, what a coincidence.

♉ They are all sitting on the sofa, he and his two most faithful companions, the ones I know best, one on his left, the other on his right, listening to him:

himself at thirty-nine and at twenty-eight, one resigned, the other angry. All three dress in the style in vogue before the war.

—I hadn't written the last syllable yet. I left the word unfinished, put my coat on, turned around and left. I didn't talk to anyone, I'll never return to that purgatory. It took a long time, but at last the day has come: I'm a free man for the rest of my life.

I Free means: without commitments. Will she accept our break-up? If we got married, she would take all the pictures she keeps in the living room to the new house, documenting the changes in her face, the duration and end of her agony. How could I live among all these eyes, hairdos, smiles and jewelry, I who am inclined to unity, who do all I can to remain whole and live in the present, without straying into the past or allowing invaders from another time to perturb the rigorous wholeness of the person I would like to be or am?

—Thirty long years of work. I've earned my reward.

—You certainly have.

—Thirty years are not thirty days!

—How well I know it.

(Activity, among insects, is limited by external changes; sleep, in such a diverse and large group, does not connote rest. Like acrobats spending the night on a trapeze or on a rope sixty feet above the ground, that is how they sleep, alert, in the same attitude they assume when they are awake).

—What are you going to do with your time now? With your freedom?

—A lot of things. I only have to choose.

♉ It is the old man speaking. The two next to him look at him from their remote ages. I hear a creaking of hinges, of ball bearings around an unlubricated axle in the young one. In some unidentified part of the body of the other one, the 39-year-old, a grooved pulley is obstinately working, cubic weights come and go in the dark. Says the younger man: "The sea is roaring." The pulley stops: "It continues to erode Milagres beach." I interpose: "Where there were houses a year ago now only their foundations and a few scattered bricks remain!" They all assent: "It's true." Silence falls again and the three of them look at me, clearly without seeing me, distressed by the encumbrance of their souls of sawdust, of bent spoons, of dull knives, channel locks and trap doors. One night ten of them came: they sat around the room—on the sofa, the six chairs, the piano bench, all angry, engaged in an excited conversation about iron bars and gates. Unfortunately, it is mostly these three who come to see me. The sixty-year-old makes me think of a zoo full of dead animals, and yet still open to the public. But one night I saw him at seventeen. He filled the room with noise, told the story of the first woman he slept with, listened to me. I have waited for his return for more than four years. I wish I could see him again, ardent and sensitive, a little perverse maybe, with his accompaniment of cymbals and bells.

—I didn't even finish writing *sixty*. I put my coat on and left. Like someone who's going to get a glass of milk. I even left the drawers open: not one thing in the office belonged to me. I would have liked to investigate the problem of the windows to the end. But, for once, I acted with determination. I got up, pushed my chair aside and left. It was exactly 9:52 when I walked through the door.

—How sad to leave like that.

—I don't see why.

♉ The youth, on his right, gets up, fastens all the chains inside himself, slams the doors, turns all the keys in their locks, which crack with rust.

—I can't stop thinking about those windows. It's a fascinating problem. Just listen to this. Originally the glazing, set in frames of anoded aluminum, was supposed to be made with three-millimeter-thick sheets of glass between which glass wool mixed with a special resin would be placed. But the wool fibers rendered the surface irregular, so a couple of panes called *Calorex-Athermane*, isolated by cotton impregnated with melanin-formol, were used instead. And how were the panes fixed in the frames? Putty is what is commonly used, but it's not very effective. So, even though the glass was anti-thermic, they proceeded as if changes of temperature could affect it and used an elastic neoprene packing. This product has had excellent results in large buildings, abroad. So far, so good. Not too long after this, the humidity spots began to appear on all ten floors. If you lifted the neoprene slightly, you

could see the water that had accumulated in the chan-
nels. The spatial distribution of the spots was irregular, it was impossible to discover a preference for any
one side of the building. Whereas in the broken sheets
of glass, yes: there was a preference indeed. A rhythm.
What clue to follow to solve this puzzle? Investigating
it fascinated me. It was the first time in almost thirty
years that I had received an assignment of some interest. I looked at the *Calorex-Athermane* as if they were
animals, victims of some epidemic. Glass cats or horses.
You know how much I disliked my boss. The more I
was tempted not to retire until I discovered the real
cause of the spots and the cracked glass, the more I
hated him.

♉ I look at my portraits on the wall. Time corrodes
and destroys people's faces. Time and this man wore
mine out. Time wrinkled my forehead, he put these
dark circles under my eyes; time took my teeth, he
gave my mouth this crooked grimace; time made my
profile emaciated, he engraved on my face this expression of defeat; together they filled the empty depths of
my soul with rust and mold.

—You talk as if you were very fond of cats and horses,
Mendonça. As if you were capable of raising a finger
for any living creature.

—Why not? On hot nights, I open the window in my
room and lie on the bed. Moths fly in, at times even
beetles. I don't kill them. I'm glad to see them.

—Because they're made of wire, mica, scraps of copper. And they have glass eyes. After working for thirty years, you didn't even have anyone to hug good-bye.

—Hug them, why? They weren't my friends.

—Someone must have been.

—Nobody was. Nobody.

♉ On his left, the obscure pulley heaves again and the voice of this gray-headed Mendonça commends him without hesitation:

—You did very well. That's how I thought I'd finish my career, twenty-one years ago. You did very well. Why say good-bye to those worthless people?

(The flies, quite a few of them sometimes, seem paralyzed, as if they were dead, covered with a fine whitish dust. Small fungi, as they devour the insects' tissue, disseminate their deadly spores. The smallest current of air carries them to the flies that are still uncontaminated. The fungi grow, invade them, eat away their tissue, destroy all the organs. The sick flies renounce flying. They passively sit on a wall, on a sheet of paper, on an armchair, on top of a file cabinet. Soon, all that is left of what they were is their shell, the void appearance, invaded by tenuous filaments).

—If only we had gotten married! Or lived together, as so many do.

—Don't talk like that, Giselda.

—Our children would be over twenty by now.

—You know that my salary was small. Then my father died. Should I have abandoned my mother?

—Of course not. Since all of your brothers were

married, you had to sacrifice. She needed someone to torment so much! Only God knows what that poor man went through. He told me about it more than once. He used to say that because his wife's name was Maria José, she wanted to be both Maria and José at the same time. He was right.

—It was unfair of him to say that. Especially to a stranger.

—I wasn't a stranger. The first time he talked about it we had been engaged over eleven years. And you were making good money.

♉ The three of them sitting on the sofa again, one next to the other. The hinges, weights, pulley, bolts, ball bearings are creaking inside them. The 39-year-old raises his right hand to his mouth:

—Perhaps it was my fault. All this aridity. It wasn't too late to change. I had some savings, didn't I? I could have quit my job, married you, gotten the shop started, made wrought iron bars and gates. What did I do instead?

♉ The young man enumerates with his head hanging :

—You started to cross out those boxes. What a masterpiece, those checkered rectangles 32 by 16 inches. 3,200 squares: 3,200 days. This was your contribution. At the end of each work day, a cross would be placed on a square, three on Fridays, two the day before a holiday. To keep track of the days that were left before retirement. At this time, there was already very little of me left in you.

—I had eleven years of service. That was the difference. In a job you—not I—obtained, by dint of entreaties and recommendations. Don't forget that.

—But not to spend my whole life there. Not to spend over thirty years. Crosses on a piece of paper! I wanted to make iron artifacts, that was my dream. And you…All this makes me feel like crying. To cross out little boxes! After a while those years began to look like a cemetery.

—You talk as if anyone could be happy to see days die like that. But it was all done out of anger. I hated it as much as you did.

—What was the use of this dead anger? A prisoner is freer than that. He thinks about ways of escaping, sizes up the height of the walls, the strength of the bars, tries to find out if the guards can be bribed. He doesn't limit himself to counting the days of his term. You two crossed the boxes out and that was all. You thought you were different from the others. And maybe you were, but not in anything important. Like all of them, you never had the courage to take any risks. It all revolved around retirement income, bonuses, surtax, fees, overtime, *prolabore,* incomes, commission, advance, due date, stipend, remuneration, salary, cash compensation, promotion, breaks and retirement.

(Some parasites invade anthills and eat all of the larvae—not even the eggs escape their voracity. They decimate the colonies they have invaded by secreting a honey that instead of nourishing the ants intoxicates them. Oblivious to everything else, they devote themselves to the invaders. Others become the slaves of warrior ants. They serve the conquerors, feed them, tend their enemies' eggs. But they themselves do not reproduce).

—Your mother always tried to pass for a martyr. A saint. I never saw anyone more preoccupied with having an angelic appearance. She should have smelled better to pull it off. Her clothes always smelled like a wet dog.

—That's not true.

—It was your father who told me. The comparison is his. She never knew anything, poor innocent. Her head was always tilted to one side, like one of those cheap religious images, her hands clasped in her lap. She didn't know a thing about the most notorious scandals. So she could pretend that she didn't meddle with other people's business and hear once more, with new details, what she already knew. Always feigning surprise.

—In any case, she was a good woman and affectionate with me. When I went to bed, she'd put cotton in my ears to keep the ants from getting in. She insisted that I get married. All she asked was not to be left alone.

—She knew that no woman could stand that. Nobody could compete with her when it came to tormenting people without appearing to do so. I was there, one day, when your father asked where he could find the sulfur powder; he had hives. Instead of telling him where she had hidden the medicine, she sat down and spent half an hour talking about leprosy. Ever so sweetly. Then she got up, changed, put on her shoes and went to church. Without even combing her hair.

—This is not the way to talk about the dead.

♉ We can see the ridge poles of the houses and the steeples of the churches, from here; St. Francis' cloister, empty, with the seraphic orb adorning the wooden ceiling; the carved stones of the Carmo church; the two-faced eagle with its wings spread in front of the pulpit, in the charity hospital. In the southeast, bathed in moonlight, is Recife, its houses built on the islands and the plain and spilling into the hills all around. The lighthouse beacon revolves with the rigor of the planets, the sea goes on destroying the houses at Milagres.

—How many times have you made this daily trip between Recife and Olinda, Mendonça? Don't you have a paper to mark these trips with crosses too? Your mother died three and a half years ago. What's the obstacle now? You've been coming to see me for twenty years without a reason.

—To tell you the truth, I haven't gotten used to the idea of getting married yet. All these years of life in common with her...

—Why did you get engaged to me, then? Have I wasted my life waiting for you?

♉ A scarab appears in the room, flies over my portraits, I hits the picture of Giselda in her thirties, falls to the floor on its back, tries to turn over. ♉ We both stop talking, look at its membranous wings, of an almost phosphorescent blue. Another, and yet another, come from the corridor, both orange, with small black spots. The first one begins to fly again, they all fly into each other, hit the chairs, the lamp, the wall, the top of the piano, go out through the window. I With a shudder, Giselda clasps her hands.

—I can't help it: I've been afraid of those insects since I was a child.

—What would happen if you saw one of those insects that live in caves, with no eyes, and antennae bigger than their body?

—I don't even want to think about it.

—Or African processionary ants. They wander through savannas and forests, devouring plants and animals. Even the trees flee, filled with fear.

—Stop, please.

—It's an issue nobody can ignore. We are in the era of insects: 750,000 to one million animal species. Airplanes combed the sky with fine nets at an altitude between 12,000 and 60,000 feet, where the air is purer and emptier. They caught 36 million insects. 36 million, Giselda. This fact led me to formulate a hypothesis for the case of the broken glass. I think they are the cause.

—Who?

—Some species of insects that I might have eventually identified. The cracks were only on the external sheets, that is, in the *Calorex* glass. Whereas when the internal ones, the *Athermanes*, were defective, it was because of what's called "accidental mechanical impact." Now, there is nothing, with the exception of a bureaucrat perhaps, whose reactions are more constant and predictable than an insect's.

—That's right, Mendonça. And you are an example of it, even though you believe the contrary. During the first years at work, you looked at your colleagues as if they were exposed to an illness you were immune to. As if it were possible to be around infected people without running any risk. You talked about the gates you'd make, about the balcony railings, about the wrought iron planters. We sat at the table, next to each other, I embroidering our trousseau, you sketching the objects you planned to make. Suddenly, I would hear a noise like wall clocks make before they give the hour. It was you, busy engendering another being in your entrails, not a man, something else, a fibroma of straw and twine, with its limited and sacred vocabulary: requisitions, forms, applications, reports, instructions, items and paragraphs.

—Perhaps you're right. One thing I managed to do, though: think. I did everything I had to do, but with my hands only. Inside, detached from my activity, I laughed at these obligations. There are insects that can survive without their head for up to a year. All my colleagues are like that. Not me. Don't compare me to them. I hate and despise those poor of spirit, who attach more importance to instructions than to themselves. They all gave up thinking; the regulations think for them. When they sit down at their desks, they feel that they represent the Institution, almost in the same sense the pope represents the Church. They're untouchable and don't make mistakes. Through them the code becomes action, something blind and concrete at the same time. A sentence. Every ruling, every stamp, every seal, is a necessary and inflexible sentence, an act that must be executed perforce and that nobody can violate with impunity. That's why I latched onto the assignment concerning the windows. The spots had shapes that didn't look like seals or stamps. And who knows if through this job I might not also be able to resurrect whatever good I had in me?

(Wasps poison peccaries and take them to their nests, paralyzed. Their larvae eat only large living game. If, after having dug a tunnel, buried the peccary, and hatched their eggs between its bristles, they find at the entrance another animal like the one they just left behind, they will open the tunnel again, only to close it when the buried peccary is exposed, then re-opening it once more upon seeing the unburied one, repeating this game until exhaustion, incapable of perceiving that there is one buried animal and another above ground.)

—The cracks in the windows of the building didn't show a preference for a given direction or a regular distribution. But there was an order, a mechanism, a rhythm reminiscent of the behavior of insects: on all floors, from the first to the tenth, there was a higher incidence of broken windows in the eastern part of the north side; in the northern part of the west side; and in the western part of the south side. The number of broken windows gradually decreased in the direction opposite to each of these segments.

♉ The one with graying hair seems interested, he looks like a father encouraging his son as he works his way through the difficulties of an exam:

—What about the east side?

—The east side doesn't have any windows. But everything indicates that, if it did, the most affected would be the ones on the southern part . There may very well be a reason why the species of insects responsible for the damage to the windows had a preference for the left side of the vertical glass surfaces. In Lima there was a building in which the same phenomenon was observed. And don't bees perform a complex and exact dance, related to the position of the sun, to indicate the source of their nourishment? Similarly, insects and water could be working together to ruin the building. As an experiment, I tried to avoid the infiltration of water through the packing, sealing the edges with mastic. In some windows I had the double sheets replaced with a single *Calorex* sheet a quarter of an inch thick, fixed with neoprene or with soft Igás putty, with a baguette molding. The results? The windows that were replaced but not treated with mastic showed traces of humidity on the internal surface of the packing; the others resisted the penetration of water. But both continued to crack, at the same rate. On some of the cracked areas residues of organic matter were found. This was confirmed by laboratory tests. Then I began to read about vermin. The carriers of plague, cholera, typhoid fever, trachoma, dissentery, those that suck the sap of trees, destroy fruits, eat seeds, leaves, roots, the enemies of domestic animals, those that invade continents and flagellate entire regions. I didn't find any reference to a kind that would destroy glass. But I learned one thing that stunned me. They resist all and any toxic substance and will one day be the masters of the earth. It's not without reason that you shudder every time you see a beetle.

☿ What does it matter, if I will not exist anymore then, and will leave no offspring? I was riding a bus, when I saw the bird: it flew over the grass and toward the church. It was on that day that the boy appeared, his bells merrily jingling in the cold silence of this room. Mendonça and I were holding hands; we had been sitting like that for a long time, without talking, and without feeling the other's hand anymore. Then he appeared, just like those beetles a short while ago—Mendonça at seventeen. He walked in smiling, opened the piano, ran his fingers across the keyboard, asked if we were going to get married. Mendonça did not seem to see him, I answered that we were, offered him a glass of liqueur.

—You two are too old to start anything.

☿ It was then that I realized the futility of my life, in a flash. I had been engaged for twenty-four years and had no intention of marrying this man anymore. My decision had been made. And I did not even know it.

—I wonder what happened to Raquel.

☿ I heard, coming from within the man, whose eyes, full of spite and disgust, were fixed on the boy, the sound of a spring snapping and vibrating, a muffled creaking of screws, of nails being pulled out. He answered in an almost inaudible voice:

—I don't know any Raquel.

—What do you mean, you don't? Think about it. It was the year right after the War, when the annual festival of the Carmo church was resumed. The worship of the image in the niche of the façade. Everybody kneeling on the slabs of the church plaza, at night, reciting the rosary. How can you not remember? She was next to you. You were pretending to be praying. When she smiled, you thought: "She's a prostitute." And you began to tremble. You still hadn't known a woman.

☿ Next to me, the metallic sound had become quite clear and more alarming: sheets of zinc rattling in the wind.

—He hadn't, Giselda. It was she who took his hand and said: "Let's go." They walked down Camboa do Carmo like two lovers, turned on Travessa de São Pedro, crossed the Pátio, went into the bushes, took off their clothes. She laid her dress out on the grass. He was worried about snakes, but lay down. When the girandole exploded, Mendonça was sitting up, and only then saw the woman's body, lying on the ground. He bent over, Giselda, and kissed those feet covered with dust. Then it started to rain. He lay down again and said: "Let's stay here, Raquel. We're going to be born in the rain, like seeds."

—Did they make love again?

—Yes, they made love again.

♉ His story had filled me with excitement. But I did not know if it was the tale or Mendonça himself who communicated to me the ardor of adolescence. His joy transformed everything, the furniture looked newer, the living room brighter, the piano resounded when he raised his voice. Even his treachery shone like a sun. Then I remembered the bird—I had forgotten about it—and I thought I should recount such an unusual and simple event. I am on the bus. As it passes the college of the Holy Family, a bird glides over the glass and, rising higher, flies toward the rose window of the chapel. With the motion of the bus, there is a moment, a fraction of a second in which the stained glass window blazes, reflecting the sun, in a brief and blinding palpitation. In the center of this flame, suspended for an instant, is the bird. Blinded, I can no longer see it, and I have the impression that it was consumed by that pulsation, swallowed or burnt to ashes by the incandescent glass.

—We can find ways of protecting ourselves from the water, Giselda. But not from insects. It's precisely because they are so small that they have enormous possi-

bilities of survival. They quench their thirst with a drop
of water; they survive floods on a straw. There is only
one hope: the extinction of many species was preceded
by a tendency to gigantism. Growth, for them, is a more
dangerous enemy than birds, frogs and reptiles. No
kind of mimetism will protect them when they are
larger. And a lot of insects are growing. We found two
dragonflies squashed against a window. Their wings,
full of nervures as big as veins, were larger than a
swallow's.

♉ The two past Mendonças, so quiet today, get up,
take leave of me. It is always like this: this Mendonça
and the others never leave or arrive together, and they
never show up alone. On the threshold, the younger
one turns to the other:

—It's not the insects that will invade the earth. Bu-
reaucrats will, Mendonça. Just imagine what a world.
Not a soul to say good-bye to, after thirty years.

♊ She closes the door, sits in front of me. In compact
formations, veritable clouds as big as a city, some, without apparent reason, cross the seas, covering thousands
of miles until they disperse. Some species do not eat
during the migration, driven by an urge stronger than
anything else and made up of all the urges that constitute their nature: eating, mating, resting, all is turned
into motion. The flitting of their gray wings can be
heard in the distance. I no longer know what Giselda's
face looks like, nor will I find it in these pictures where
it has dissolved, with a lock falling over her forehead

(à la Clara Bow?), with black bangs, then red, with arched eyebrows, frightened eyes, part of the face hidden by blond hair, and the corners of the mouth turned down, imitating some celebrity, her latest idol, the last imaginary link with an ideal universe in which she longed to live even after her youth was gone.

—Do you think that time creates obligations, Giselda?

—I think that when you have no substance, everything becomes a pretext for denials. You were a failure.

—Should I have investigated the problem of the windows? Until I found a solution?

—You really should have become attached to someone. Or something. You've been living like some nut who spends twenty, thirty years in a station, without ever making up his mind whether to take a train or go back home.

—If this is what you think of me, I think I should leave.

—I've wanted to break off this engagement for four years. From the day I saw you at seventeen. Do you remember?

—No.

—I told you the story of the bird that flew up to the rose window and disappeared in the blaze of glass. You were looking at me, with the eyes of a child, almost, as if I hadn't reached the end yet. Then you got up and hit him. It was as if you had shaken a bunch of bells, as if you had struck silver pipes. Don't you remember? Neither of you was crying or groaning. You opened the door and left with your bells, and you, you cursed, took your hat and left without saying good-bye, with a dozen pulleys—or were they hornets?—whirring in your heart of sawdust. Don't you remember?

—No. Nothing like that ever happened.

—I remained alone, still hearing that silvery sound echoing in the corridor, and I said to myself that I would not marry you, and that only the hope of seeing you again at seventeen would keep me from breaking off the engagement. You've aged so much, Mendonça! Why do I only hear the clanging of iron tools in your soul now?

(Insects look like the creation of some idle and imaginative genius. Spherical bodies shaped like wood chips, seeds, coins, their heads elongated like knives, apterous, with wings spread or encrusted on their back, equipped with pincers, borers, stingers, mandibles, faceted eyes, antennae, their legs short, or long, or countless, black or colored, mute, voices of the Night, singers of Summer, useful, predators, inhabitants of the waters, of the surface or of the depths, of the air, they, more than any other living species, sound the possibilities of the world).

—All these years of resentment must have killed the best in me.

—There are no more inexpugnable cities. But a man, to be ransacked, must open the gates.

—Maybe I wasted my energies in the effort I made to protect myself. I didn't want to become associated with those people. I wasn't like them and I detested what they were. I thought. I thought up to the end, and the Boss knew. He knew I despised all mechanical gestures. That is why he assigned the problem of the windows to me. But I realized it was a trap and left. I put my coat on, pushed the chair aside...

— You don't need to put your coat on now. Nor push the sofa aside. It's not necessary to say good-bye either.

♉ Two spiders come out of Mendonça's mouth, crawl down his shoulder, jump to the floor, a cricket begins to sing. Moths circle around the lamp. Buzzing, a cloud of mosquitoes flies in from the open window. A caterpillar climbs on the closed shutter, grasshoppers land on the sofa and on the mirror frame. Outside the window I see a praying mantis looking at us. Three enormous beetles fly in, buzzing. Red ants come in from under the door and move toward my room in a procession. A large blue butterfly flutters above us. I feel a centipede crawling up my left leg.

—You won't see me again, Giselda. At any age.

♉ He passes me, with his noise of chains dragging, of barbed wire piercing cattle skin, of hammock hooks moaning under the weight of corpses rocked by the wind. I close my eyes and remember the merry din whose return I awaited in vain all these years, school bells, rattles, maracas, the sound of wind-up toys, children's swings rhythmically creaking among shady mango boughs.

Lost and Found

Álvaro de Souza Melo Filho,
Antônio A. Macedo Lima,
Ernâni Bezerra,
Lauro de Oliveira e
Roderico Queiroz.

THE BEACH is a no man's land that the waters surrender and reclaim. Governed by the cycle of the tides, the creatures which in the beginning lived in the sea and now inhabit this frontier have long accepted the hapless condition of being fought over by the thalassic and terrestrial worlds. If some dig tunnels to escape the invasion of the rising tide, others cling to pebbles, lie still among damp stones, take refuge in tide pools. Some absorb excess water and will dry up and die if they are exposed to the sun too long. The creatures that live inside shells shut them tight; many burrow into the damp sand. The tide rises, invades the tunnels, floods their inhabitants, brings in the big fish, agile reapers, alert eye and greedy tooth. When everything has been turned over, the ebb tide comes, the loud crashing noise of the waves subsides, the fish leave. Then, upon the anemones hidden among the rocks, upon the small mollusks and crustaceans which have taken shelter in the dead waters of the beach, upon the fugitives of the countless tunnels surfacing, full of fear, among empty shells and debris spat out by the sea, then, more ravenous than the fish, descend the shadows of the coastal birds—sharp beaks, terrestrial eyes.

—Where's my son?
—I don't know.
—How old is he?
—A little over seven, blond, green trunks.
—No, I haven't seen him.
—He was here only ten minutes ago, playing with a ball.

∅ Sitting there in the sand in my swimming suit, next to the big blue canvas tent we—the clubmembers—put up two and a half hours ago, I watch Renato, three meters away from me, as he says the last sentence. He is barefoot, in black trunks and a red shirt, holding his right hand out to show the height of the boy. Is it because I have lost so many precious things, and I do not have the strength to live through what I have received in exchange, that a bitter joy, spongeful of honey and ammonia, fills my mouth? Remembering the night in which I was stripped, one by one, of everything I had with me, only to lose even more cherished possessions later, I watch his face crack with a sharp sound, the way framed sheets of glass do on days of intense heat.

∇ Lying in the sand, the color of sand myself, beneath the umbrella with yellow sections, I observe the man sitting in the shade of the tent. When the other one inquired about the child, some mechanism began to work in his eyes, suddenly transformed into piercing instruments completely devoid of compassion, like the eyes of animals of prey. I barely remember my father, I only saw him a few times, perhaps his real home was the small or medium-sized ships he sailed, his visits were not very frequent, nor long, but he looked at everything the same way: as if he were about to pounce on it. A strange face. It was worth seeing at least once in your life.

⊘ Watch him. As much as possible, follow all his steps and words with the utmost rigor, record the evolution of his despair. Observe, like a condensed version, in a few minutes, what sooner or later happens to everybody, but usually over a period of years: the realization that something essential has been snatched from us. He is still very far from this. Hesitant, one face gazing at the sea, another searching the avenue, two more trying to look as far as possible down the sun-drenched beach full of tents, swimmers and vendors, his mind, overcome by the idea that his son is dead, and comforted by the fleeting hope that he will soon find him again, resembles the beach, which the waves reclaim and surrender, then invade again. Embarrassed by his own question, because asking is like divulging his fear and giving it substance, he approaches various people, smiling, holding out his hand where the top of his son's hair would be, but the answers are always discordant, one pointed north, another south, there were vague gestures, negative answers, someone holds his arm out toward the sea.

⊚ In the same way that a droning sound born in the heart of many other noises passes through them, without history or destiny, I will appear on my bicycle, pedaling slowly along the beach, the high waves on my left, on the right the cars in the avenue, the buildings, the consulates with their big flags hoisted. I will violate, among curses, the area where the young men are playing soccer, I will see the jangada sailing rafts at sea and ashore, the ships at anchor, the motorboats, the woman swimming among the waves, children floating inside plastic animals, old men drifting in their inner tubes, the jets performing acrobatics in formation; I will pass vendors selling their baskets of mangabas, braids of cashew fruits, coconut stands, clusters of tangerines, soda and ice cream carts, parasols, straw mats, towels, wicker baskets, couples playing paddleball, groups with a feather shuttlecock, volleyball teams, sunbathers lying in the sand or swimming, other bicycles, hats in the shape of dahlias, cones, birds, boxes, lovers writing in the sand, mothers chastising their progeny, children looking for shells or making sand castles. I will pass through it all, I will record it all, completely unnoticed, before I vanish the same way a buzzing sound ends, never to be remembered again.

—Hi, Renato. How's it going?

—OK, I guess.

—What do you think of the planes?

—I wasn't paying attention to them. I'm worried about...

—Did you ever get to see the Zeppelin ?

—Just the picture. It came out in the papers.

—I was very young then, but I remember. That was really something. I wonder why they don't still make zeppelins.

—Me too. My son...

—That's right...everything changes. Just think what our children will see.

—Where are yours?

—Over there, in the water.

—Did any of them want to see the Independence Day parade?

—No.

—Mine did. He loves parades. You haven't seen him around, have you?

—No. Mine took after me. They like mechanics and the beach. Shall we go in the water?

—Later.

—Why later? It's 11:40. In half an hour the bus will be here. We don't have much time. Let's go. They say life began in the sea. Let's return to our origins.

∧   It began in the sea? Where exactly, if ancient mountains lie under the oceans and marine skeletons are sometimes found at great altitudes? I do not know how I could give in to his insistence, even though he did insist a lot, and how I can be swimming now, when

I cannot see my son, when nobody is telling me anything about him, when maybe he is only a few meters
away from me, face down in the sand. Throughout the
long Cambrian Period the earth was uninhabited: life
was present only in the water, which was fishless. No
vertebrates. Mollusks, sponges, jellyfish, long trilobites
drifted, sounding the marine depths. The swimming
animals had not appeared yet. Bald, sterile and dead,
as in times not even fossils can remember, that is how
I see the earth now, without my son. I must get out of
the water, shout, run up and down the beach, accept
once and for all the condition of a man upon whom
the beak and claws of misfortune have descended, so
that everybody will know and help me. Even if this
search may be in vain.

∅ Do adversities come crashing down upon men's
heads? No, we plunge into them, in our blindness, like
someone who throws himself into an abyss. We are
never extraneous to the things that befall us. Could I
imagine, when I took my daughters out for a stroll on
Sunday afternoons, and picked poppies from the brick
walls for them, or sat in the grass with a volume of
Horace while they played in the sun, could I imagine
then that I was already moving toward the still remote
moment in which I would suddenly lose them? And
how could I guess, upon leaving home that afternoon,
to celebrate z.i.'s birthday in secret, that I would lose
everything, salvaging little besides my own life and
receiving in exchange something my half-heartedness

does not allow me to accept? Completely unaware of everything, I added weight and purpose to my movements, carefully preparing, step by step, that catastrophe, without even realizing that I was in the midst of a disaster when it had already been consummated. Destiny carefully conceals its machinations, and to discover them it is almost always necessary to peel away many layers of ignorance. Ahead of Renato, I ripped them away faster than anyone else: I precede him in the knowledge of his destitution. Experienced, wise, yet merciless, I will follow him as he struggles not to accept what has happened. Like an invader in the antechamber of the future, I will wait for him, alert, I will not miss a single step. He will forget almost everything he has done or will do in the next moments: the conversation about dirigibles, his extemporaneous swim, everybody's indifference, all this running around: he goes to the left, retraces his steps immediately, rushes off to the right, stops, raises his hands to his face (the first gesture of affliction), climbs to the top of the sandbank and surveys the festive beach, then starts toward a child playing in the distance, only to realize that it is not his; which exacerbates his movements, followed by a moment of stupor, then a sudden progression toward the evidence. I will record in detail his goings in the darkness, his comings. Who knows if this will not help me? He is walking toward the jangadas.

▽ Our father, who also disappeared in the sea, never saw his last child, born three weeks after his death.

The captain of the cargo ship comes to see us: "He was a good swimmer, despite his age. He must have gotten dizzy, stumbled. Anyone can have an accident. We looked for him, it was a beautiful day. Only ten minutes earlier he'd been seen paring his nails with a knife, between the deck and the lifeboats. We looked for him quite a bit. I decided to come in person to give you my condolences. If I can do anything..." That is why I know what this man's search is like. He has not given the alarm yet. Silently—or talking to himself—he is tracing concentric ellipses, widening his search around the area where he first noticed the child's absence and which in his mind has taken on the function of the imaginary center of his anxiety. That is how I picture the cargoship, describing a spiral with its bow, because of my father dead in the Atlantic. All his papers disappeared with him; the administration did not keep any pictures, and we did not have any at home either. Twenty years later, my brother, compelled to fix on a face his sudden love for the father he had never seen, would begin another search; for a picture he had learned existed in Serinhaém, Goiana and Flores do Indaiá, my father's birthplaces where half a century earlier he had received his first communion with several other children. This event had been captured on a sepia-colored photograph, twenty-five boys in white, almost all dead by now.

∧ Peacefully, the jangadas have come back, all of them, from the open sea. And my son sucked in by the waves? After the Cambrian, as big as men, and even bigger, came the marine scorpions. They multiplied, established their reign in the salty depths. They swam slowly, with their legs apart, like big aggressive seraphim. Millions of years later, the cycle of their flagellating passage consummated, they moved to salty or fresh waters and, their powers already declining, sought refuge in estuaries, rivers, lakes and lagoons. By the Permian they had disappeared. But in the previous era, when the marine fauna had become diversified and amphibious fish dragged themselves across the bottom of swamps, they still dominated. This sea which perhaps has already taken my son is for me like the waters after the Cambrian, filled with huge scorpions with irate stingers, looking like angels with dried-up wings.

—I'm starting to get worried. I can't find my son.

—He must be around here someplace.

—I'm going to look around with you. Should we go too?

—Where?

—Renato's son has disappeared.

—When?

—More than half an hour ago. What shall I do?

—Keep going this way; I'll look the other. Don't go alone, though.

∅ What is about to happen will be important: the disclosure and widening of the search, the precipitous onset of panic. I must witness these things. I walk down the beach with Renato, the black sea on one side, on

the other the buildings with their lilac glass, the avenue with glittering cars. There we are, side by side, in
the salt-colored sand, among people who have also lost
their children or their wristwatches, youth or opportu-
nities, courage or their teeth, their parents or their
money, confidence or an arm, ardor or assets, or their
identity, or their job, or their minds, or the way, or
strength, or life—there we are, following the scent of a
dead child. Somebody looks at his watch, 11:48, on
this same beach z.i. and I met to watch the moon rise.
I bring her roses, we have been meeting in dark and
deserted places, in a sort of sterile lyricism, for four
years. We have not even become lovers, we have limited ourselves to discussing that possibility. Our trysts
are tender and heart-rending, our kisses passionate,
dramatic our good-byes. But what have we done to
change our situation? We could not bring ourselves to
break up, nor to make a commitment. We blamed it on
our sensitivity, repeated that we would never be happy
at the price of somebody else's suffering: our passion
feeds on the indulgence with which we look at each
other. A painful game in which I am getting caught up
more and more, gradually losing sight of what is imaginary in it. z.i. did not come to the beach. Not to show
up occasionally, out of coyness or remorse, for long
expected trysts is part of the pleasant ritual we have
established. To arrive very late, thus manifesting our
hesitancy, is another ceremony. At times I have waited
two hours for z.i., only to leave in the end, or see her

come, ecstatic in both cases. We breathe cultivated pleasures and torments that do not affect us deeply. I need
z.i. to feel alive, it is indispensable to the economy of
my being that the secret encounters and the whispered
telephone calls between which weeks and even months
often pass—occur in the placid and safe stream of my
days, and that I evoke them among my family—my three
daughters, my prosaic and affectionate wife—the five of
us in the light of the lamp, around the table set with
china, silver and crystal. Alone, I watch the moon rise,
throw the roses in the sea. Not in vain: I will tell z.i. of
my gesture. Touched, she will ask me to meet her on
the bank of the canal, to celebrate her birthday, and
that will be the end of my comfortable and two-faced
existence. Renato's nerves are beginning to fail him. I
can tell from the self-assured way in which he is act-
ing, like those people who are more composed when
they are drunk than when they are sober. His despera-
tion increased, multiplied, all of a sudden walking
seemed a precarious recourse. He took a bicycle whose
owner must be in the water swimming, fell twice, finally
gained some balance, is pedaling smoothly now. I stay
here, to explain what happened in case the owner gets
here first. I will apologize to him.

   ∧ Real scorpions, ancestors of those existing nowadays and precursors of life on the deserted continents,
appeared in the Silurian. Then, out of mica, mud, re-
fracted light, darkness and salt, the fish are formed,
voracious from the beginning. They devour each other

and every millennium they are more numerous. Great convulsions transform the earth, promontories are submerged, lakes dry up. Seas empty out.

∅ The canal runs through Recife, from the Derby to Santo Amaro, like a blind and powerful animal. Slow and obstinate, it advances, goes around Boa Vista, almost in a straight line, cuts across streets, plazas, avenues, with its putrid waters, moat without end and more devastating than time. Both sides are covered with undergrowth, wild shrubs thrive, shacks proliferate. No light, except on the ten bridges: Paiçandu, Fronteiras, Derby, Amorim Park, Espinheiro, João de Barros, Maduro, Tacaruna. z.i. and I meet here many times, in the shadowy areas between those bridges, like many lovers whose silhouettes pass by, furtive, with their faces lowered, among toads, reptiles, grazing horses and clouds of mosquitoes. Renato is back. With extreme care, he puts the bicycle back without telling me anything about his expedition. His face has shattered into a thousand pieces. His eyes are glassy, his shirt in his hand, his trunks damp. Some children are playing. The ball, thrown up high, hits his shoulder. He turns, violently kicks it toward the sea, yells at the children. Then he begins to call his son's name aloud. The children, frightened, run away, he continues to throw the boy's name to the wind, asks me to do the same, I call out without conviction. That is how I call z.i., that night, watching her walk away certain that she will not turn to look at me, ever again. A siren reverberates somewhere, it is noon, the jet formation is back, they fly low over the beach, with a deafening noise, while the warships fire their cannons, the horizon fills with smoke, the simultaneous detonations shake the ground and the houses, Renato continues to shout, nobody hears his call, I stop.

▽ Two of the town's pious old women, Anita and Albertina, one of whom plays the fiddle and the organ, have the picture: our father and his companions, all in white, the extinguished candles. This is what my brother heard. In the sitting room, next to the parish church, among old furniture and a lit lamp of blue glass, he inquires about it. ▽ Mothers running after their children in the water or in the sand, dragging them by the arm, some by the ear. You can see the pride shining on their faces: they snatched their children from death. Resented words, words of fear crackle among them. ▽ The two whiteclad virgins know almost nothing, they confuse our father with other boys. One of them has gray hair, the fiddle-player's, despite her age, is still yellow, the color of old paper. Every now and then, without any reason, she bursts into a little laugh, hoarse and croaking, like a parrot or a snipe. ▽ One of the zealous mothers could not find her daughter and ran to the tent in tears, everybody rushes over, talking excitedly. A member of the club who got drunk dances around the agitated group, handing out cashew fruits that only the children will accept. ▽ The old women's walls, covered with sacred images, the fiddle case on top of a console. Both wear rosaries of white beads around their wrists. They say they never saw the picture. They limit themselves to describing to my brother our father at thirteen or fifteen, a description that could be of any other boy. The church bells strike nine, they cross themselves, the yellow-haired one cackles again. ▽ The news that a child is missing and that his corpse might suddenly appear on the beach, brought in by the waves, has spread. This part of the shore, turned into a mourning chamber, begins to empty. People talk, look toward the club's blue tent, some come to see what is going on, others have already left. ▽ The gray-haired one says to my brother that it is Jovina Veras who must have the picture with our father. But Jovina has moved, lives with a brother, on a farm. Where? They do not know exactly: out of town. They will pray that my brother finds what he is looking for. ▽ The light has risen from the ocean like a giant amphibian, emerged from the abysses. Daggers gleam among the waves. With its keels of silver, oars of fire and enormous resplendent sails, hundreds of galleys slowly move across the horizon, reflected by the sea. The amphibian has grown, is advancing, invades us, fills me with light, I close my eyes and see myself the way you see an egg against the sun. Even the lights in the closed up houses have come on, even the basements are lit up. Brief dialogues, in this light so intense and surreal that for a moment I cannot see anything: "When's the bus coming?" "In ten or fifteen minutes." "How many teeth does the Leviathan have?" "Four in the upper arch, twelve in the lower, twenty-four in the middle." "What about Renato? Shall we wait for him?" "Of course not." ▽ The sulphur-haired woman cackles again. The other has placed a drawer next to the lamp, and is showing us the pictures she has. Daughters of Mary grouped around the vicar, death notices, Guy de Fontgalland, white dresses, black dresses, high boots, curls, wicker scats, iron gates, dogs, chairs, bouquets. She doesn't know the names of these ghosts, does not recognize anyone. The fiddler has also bent over the pictures, but cannot add anything to her sister's uncertainties. They weep, the two old maids, over that world they have witnessed and of which they know so little. "We can't remember anything. You can have the pictures if you like." ▽ The morning quivers with explosions and lamentations. A piercing constellation, seven airplanes slice through the winds. Bottles, dishes, cups and glasses dance in the cupboards, knives and ladles rattle in the drawers, clocks stop, pictures swing in their hooks, crystals shatter. The relationship between the fuselage of airplanes and the deafening noise filling land and sea seems to me identical to that existing between the bill of a peacock and the fan of its feathers.

There is, fringing this no man's land, a strip which is never uncovered by the waters, as low as the tide may be. A fauna of indolent beings, averse to adventure and reluctant to change, undecided between animal and plant, sea and continent, has inhabited it for millions of years. A fish invades this archaic and mortal land, covered with long vibratile cilia, with tentacles like ferns and heads like calices. Suddenly, it is pierced by arrows and can no longer move. The killer does not come out in the open: it waits until the waters carry the victim within reach of its apathy and, without hurrying, brings it to the opening which serves as a mouth. Sometimes it happens that animals once vital come to this sad zone and here multiply. They lose their agility, color, initiative, skeleton. They take pleasure in imitating the indolence of anemones and jellyfish, with time they begin to resemble them and eventually become indistinguishable. They cast off everything, seek nothing more.

∧ The plants of the earth, preparing the terrain for the coming of animals, appear in the Devonian. My friend Albano has just arrived, I see the fenders of his bicycle. He does not greet me.

—What is it, Renato?

—I don't know what to do any more. He's gone.

∧ Deep lakes and big lagoons formed at that time. The first insects, similar to fleas, leaped in the silence, lords of the birdless spaces.

—Where did you see him last?

—That's the problem. I can't remember.

∧ Those who went to look for my son at the other end of the beach have already returned. In the Carboniferous, the trees and the giant insects grow, beetles, ants, forests proliferate, butterflies with wings as big as palm-leaf fans graze in the prairies.

—I can't remember. I think it was when he was playing in the sand; but then again, it seems that he called to me and I didn't turn.

—How could you let him out of your sight with a sea like this!

∧ The sea claimed again the land it had lost, fish swam among tree branches, other forests were conquered, drowned, became petrified. The fish were the birds of those black woods.

—It just happened.

—Go get dressed.

∧ Many people have already changed their clothes and are sitting in the sun or in the shade of the tent. Is it that late? Soon they will all leave. I will be alone.

—When?

—Now. We're going to the police station.

—It's a waste of time. (The glaciers and the deserts). My heart tells me that he's dead. (The reptiles evolve in the Permian). What have I done to deserve this?

∅ The naive question. The same one z.i. asked so many times, when the situation in which we lived, torn as we were between adventure and doubt, seemed to cloud her mind. "Before meeting you, I lived in peace with my husband and children, they were my whole life. I haven't done anything to deserve this misery, this exhausting dream. I don't know for what sins I was condemned to nourish this cancer within me." "Nothing keeps you from leaving me." "You know that

I can't. I'm expiating some evil deed." In the tent, Renato
gets dressed to continue his search. Why should human destiny be a punishment or a reward? A fire burns
down the walls and roof of the just man, all his children die. The floods wash away plantations irrigated
with honest sweat, hard work and prayers. The sinner's
fortune grows larger and, in his old age, after a short
and placid end, his children and wife bemoan his death.
Life does not give any marks for good behavior. What
appears to be justice is only disorder and chance. There
must be a God, since the Devil exists. Does this mean
that I must see in what happened to me a sentence, a
punishment, the wrath manifested by some sovereign
entity? The bus has just arrived. Before it turned
around, a lot of people got on and took all the seats.
For a man in this condition, going in and out of the
tent, looking at the bus, perplexed, maybe even hiding
in the dressing room preparing himself for some difficult
act carried out with modesty, this is like facing a
dreaded goodbye. As long as familiar even though
indifferent faces surround him he can fool himself or
his fear. When they leave, he will have to face his despair. He will find himself alone and his misfortune
will seem like a handicap, something like the gangrene
that forces fugitives to abandon a man to the wolves
or the ants. That is how I feel that night, on the bank
of the canal—gangrenous, with nobody by my side, waiting to be thrown into the stagnant water.

   ▽ The blue tent measured four meters by three,

and it was three meters high. Once the canvas was rolled up around the poles, and the ropes and iron hooks were gathered, a void opened up. A few people are still standing around the man who lost his son, and who is now wearing sunglasses; most of them got on the bus, the driver is honking impatiently. A few couples, more affluent perhaps, brought their own umbrellas and set them up far from the others, so they would not look as if they had come to the beach with everybody else. They approach looking very distinguished (or so they think), the men carrying fishing gear under their arms, the women wearing colorful straw hats. They march on, haughty and full of disdain, indifferently pass the man with the sunglasses, ignoring the honking and the square of empty space left by the tent. Our father, when he is at home, during the intervals between his travels, works as a cooper. He shapes the oaken staves with care, fastens them with strips of steel. When he leaves, the tools and the materials he works with remain in the yard. His presence, like his absence, has the same forest smell. Which is also the smell of his voice, of his unexpected arrivals, of his sudden goodbyes, the smell of noise and silence, of death and ships. When we are told that he will not be coming back, our mother gets rid of the tools, sells the leftover steel and wood. Then the yard dies: and it is in this emptiness that the man with the tense expression on his face really disappears for me. From repeating so many times to my brother, who demands more and more details, that look, the face, the body and the voice of our father, I lose him. His memory, upon which my own words as well as my brother's desires or suppositions begin to impinge, dies out little by little. Thus, because of his eagerness, my brother destroys the only clear image of our father. All that is left to me is the expression of his eyes (not the color, not even the shine or the shape) and the oak smell in the yard. As for our mother, she was never able to talk about her husband. To the point that I sometimes wonder if she actually ever saw him.

—You're really leaving, then?

—I'll make an announcement on the radio, if you want.

—It's not necessary. Are you coming with me, Albano?

—Of course!

—It would be better to take a cab.

—I'll drive slowly. Look on both sides, maybe you'll see him.

—See you later, Renato. We'll ask the driver not to go fast. Well keep an eye out. If you find the kid, you can stop a car and catch up with the bus. If we do, we'll wait for you.

▽ Everybody has left. The two friends, each with his back turned to the other, look in opposite directions. Now they turn, exchange some words I cannot hear, they walk away. It is when invoking God's name is no longer natural for him that his plans begin to take on the aspect, in his mind, of an absurd compromise between his own forces and chance, it is when

the old certainties disappear and certain interrogatives
he did not even dare to voice before turn into dogmas,
when certain questions previously answered turn into
their own answers, it is, in short, when he loses his
faith that my brother becomes obsessed with my
father's face, to substitute it for God's, now hidden.
His search is different from this man's: it is not for
another encounter that he is preparing; he is trying to
claim the invisible, the unknown, to reach, through
intricate labyrinths, a remote being and his halo. First
I have to recreate the way in which the sailor makes
vats and tubs, shapes barrel staves, rounds the hoops
and arranges each piece: the barrel staves of the casks,
joined by the first steel band, are petals forming a big
oaken flower, which is born open and closes later,
bound by the last hoop. Then I have to evoke the instruments of an art practiced without compass or ruler,
by an expert eye and hands that know the right mea-
surements; I have to soak the wood to make it more
docile to the camber, I have to warm it up in a fire of
wood chips and compose anew the music, the rhythm
our father invents when he hammers the boards during the last phase of each piece, a rhythm subject to
countless variations, always new and always identical.
Then, my brother begins to demand that I make our
father visible to him and, with time, his questions become statements instead; he has engendered within
himself a figure born of who knows what mold, and
while he pretends to be asking, he instills in my memory

his own version of the dead. Could these two images have destroyed each other in me, like two ferocious fish or gamecocks?

⊘ One night I come to the beach with z.i., in a cab. The car moves as slowly as this bus, we are still at the beginning of our relationship, I watch her with fear. I have just felt, in her hands, a quivering, a fluttering of wings immediately suppressed. Her face, in the shade, has something of a bristling animal. ∧ In the Permian the reptiles appear, thick layers of ice cover the south of Africa. The police officer in Boa Viagem knows nothing about lost children or salamanders, none was reported to him this Sunday. During the apogee of reptiles, mollusks protected by shells appear everywhere. The design of the shells mirrors, with increasing rigor, a definite rhythm. ∇ My brother continues his search for the picture. He goes everywhere he knows or imagines there are relatives of the cooper—the seaman: Porto Real do Colégio, Igaraçu; Cabedelo, Barreiros, Coruripe; Penedo, Areia, Porto Calvo. Years of search, all in vain. ∧ A varied species and absolute lords of the plain, some on two feet, others on four, the dinosaurs dominate the planet for a hundred million years. Crocodiles, tritons, turtles, serpents and dragons go back to the sea. There are so many that the level of the water rises. In the Cretaceous flowers, the Pyrenees, the Rocky Mountains, the Caucasus, the Himalayas, the harmonious skeleton of fish bloom. ⊘ z.i. and I walk in silence, looking at the distant lights of the ships in the dark.

She brought me a bilingual edition of the *Sonnets from the Portuguese,* says she underlined E. B. Browning's verses: "I will not let you come near me, for fear you would suffer my pains." ▽ He has moved to the south of Bahia, keeps writing to all the relatives. In Serinhaém, in Goiana, in Flores de Indaiá. He asks them about the alleged picture of our father. Insistent letters, which go unanswered most of the time. ∧ Seals? Sea elephants? Walruses? Amphibious children? The police officer at Pina wrings his hands regretfully. Albano pats my back, I lower my head. Shall we come back? Shall we go on? In the ocean a cold, black saddlebag bursts open, and out of it leap all the toads and frogs that inhabit nightmares, swamps and hollow trunks, with their long hind legs, their drunken eyes, their slimy skin. Some, like silkworms, hibernate, then they break out of the cocoon, become bats, soar to the heights of the night. ▽ Our aunt writes to my brother. She found the photograph, it is in her hands. He wires: DO NOT SEND PRECIOUS FIND BY MAIL. WILL COME GET IT AS SOON AS POSSIBLE. ⊘ I kiss Z.I., it is the first time. Her mouth is as warm as a bird in the summer sun. Was there, when I kissed her, a muffled trill, the hint of a cicada song in her hips, in her shoulders? ∧ With the bats, the lemurs also venture forth. The skeletons of some beings become lighter, feathers cover their bodies, they fly in the air. Fearless fish rise above the water. Some bird, frightened by its own voice, begins to sing. ▽ The reply to my brother: "Unfortunately

I don't have the picture any more. Isabe Veras, Jovina's sister, came to take it back. She says that it's precious, because one of the children in it is in the family. She doesn't know which one. But I recognized your father. When you come, we'll go to Isabe's house together." Years pass before he comes to Pernambuco. I cannot tell whether he has come to resemble father more, or whether the face I remember as the Deceased's is actually his. ⊘ I have chosen, to celebrate z.i.'s birthdays, a different date from the day on which she was born, like the sovereigns of England. She wears a new dress, comes to meet me (always in solitary places), I give her presents, inexpensive but meaningful. ∧ Continents coalesce and separate, ice and fire appear, stones turn into rhinoceroses, wind into horses, gourds into armadillos, the shadow of foliage into tigers, dawn into lions, sponges into three-toed sloths, tree branches into deer and caribous, the earth is filled with roars, howls, whistles, neighs and bellows and suddenly there is a silence, the hour of humankind has come. ⊘ For this birthday, I bring z.i. an album with drawings of roses centered on huge sheets of paper above their Latin names, *fusca superba, corona rubrorum, gemma rubra, omnium calendarum, glauca, virginalis, scandeus, balearica, reclinata, rubra, hispida, sulphurea, corimbosa, mutabilis. Mutabilis.*

∧ And him? The eras past, the fossils of cyclones and of eruptions, the freezes and fires, the arid millennia, the floods, the cataclysms, exoduses, submerged mountains, the pulsing of blood, the trajectory of the arrow; the seed in the ground, the fruit ripening, everything happened for my son—neither a bird nor a fish—to be and cease to be? Like the earth in space, in the depths of space, atolls are born in the ocean with their illusion of tranquillity and their shipwrecks. ⊘ The bus stops, some people get off, they think they saw the boy wandering along the beach. They come back. We all turn into stone and silence.

Four hundred meters below sea level darkness begins, and the only lights are those of phosphorescent animals. The ebb and flow of the water above still reaches this darkness. Six hundred meters below all movements cease: in the heart of this invisible, obscure and dense universe creatures with cylindrical bodies, not very large, spy on each other. Their sinister eyes, placed on the sides of their head, see in all directions at the same time. Some have separated their blind eyes into threads and sound the black depths with long tactile filaments. They are all carnivore and equipped with steely teeth. If elsewhere it is the destiny of fish to be eaten by enemies of greater strength, in these abysses the law is reversed: with their enormous mouths and their dilatable bodies the pelagic creatures devour prey four times bigger than themselves.

▽ Soon I will take the umbrella apart, pick up the straw mat, oils, towel, the shade, and I will leave. Directly in front of me, bathers—men and women—excitedly exchange words and gestures I do not understand, they all run out of the water, onto the beach. They pass by me, I hear the words *leg* and *shark*. The tide comes in, the waters expand again their movable frontiers. From the ocean, from its depths, comes the continuous cry of a swallow. This bird does not exist in Pernambuco. My aunt, my brother and I around the small table, the lamp hanging above our green heads. Two candles burning in the oratory. Pictures of saints on all the walls, behind the doors, statuettes on the furniture. "Isabe Veras died a week ago. Even less." "What about the house? Her things, the pictures? Did you go there?" "It didn't occur to me." "You pray so much that you don't have time to think about anything else. You should have kept the picture." "It was hers. What could I do?" "You should have told her that you had lost it." "Maybe we can go there tomorrow. Jovina Veras may be able to help you, if she hasn't moved yet." "Didn't she live on a farm, with another brother?" "Isabe and Jovina were living together again. Had been, for many years. I'm going to find out where the house is." My brother cannot wait an entire night, he drags us around the three silent towns. We find the house, which Jovina Veras is still occupying, we bang on the door. Even our aunt knocks lightly with her bony knuckles, smiling, surprised at her own boldness. Nobody answers. My brother, bleary-eyed, like someone far away, on the other side of a wide river, looks at

the images in the oratory, blows out the two candles.
Closer, distinct, the screeching of the swallows.

∅ We had to stop for the fourth time, this time to
pick him up, and not because someone thinks he saw
his son. All he said was "No." He sits down quietly,
without looking around, his gangrene invades us. On
the bank of the canal, the album with drawings of roses
in my hand, I wait for z.i. to show up. For some of the
clandestine lovers the time of their hurried encounters
is up, they part, each goes in a different direction, on
the paths cutting through the wild growth. From the
stagnant waters rises a smell of trash, rotten fruit, human waste and burning sulphur. Two things are nag-
ging at me: the album, which I took the precaution of
hiding among my shirts, was not in the same position,
and it is already close to dinnertime, my family must
be waiting far me, I do not want to be late. If throughout these many months z.i. had not managed to incor-
porate her delays with my waits, much longer than normal, I would have left. But this pleasure—almost a vice—
she feels in always appearing to struggle with herself,
has infected me, dissolving within me that more or
less brief moment in which, our patience at an end, we
decide that the person we are waiting for will not come,
and leave. I look at my watch in the flare of the lighter.
Later than I thought. All is set for my ruin: the thickness of the night, the propitious hour, the absence of
stars, the dim reflections in the water, the pit in which
I will fall. Now at the core of the event that has been

brewing for three years, imminent the gesture for which there will be no mending, I get up, cautiously take a few steps forward on the wide wall of the canal. In the sooty field, which, in this night of few lights, is the putrid place z.i. and I transformed into a river, I make out a small roundish area to my left. I feel with my foot what I think is firm ground, lose my balance, plunge headlong into a watery world of worms and debris, sink to the bottom, flail about in that noxious paste, tumble with my arms wide while my cry gets muffled in the mud; I sink in the swamp, fall wondering why this is happening to me, roll like a stone into the darkness that invades my nostrils with its creatures and weeds. The album with the drawings of roses—the *Président Carnot,* the *Niphetos,* the *Souvenir de Wooton*— will never be found. In the almost empty bus—since many, including Renato, have joined a dismayed group of people in the center of which a child is crying, a boy everybody believes to be someone he actually is not— I await their return.

—It's not him, Renato. But this old man saw a lost child half an hour ago.

—How old was he?

—About eight. Two women were leaving in their car.

—And?

—They took him home. He knew the name of the street where he lives.

—His hair...what color was it?

—Black. Long. He was wearing something red.

—Red?

▽ My brother and I knock on Jovina's door again. We are told that she went to the city hall with her brother. We do not find her. They must have gone to the church, to take care of matters related to Isabe's death. My brother refuses to enter, I inquire in the sacristy. We find the two old people at the civil registry, she staring at the walls while he signs papers. Men in the waiting room, all looking sad, even the ones who came to register their newborn children. My brother approaches Jovina, tells her in a low voice about the picture in which our father appears. She looks at him, frightened, without understanding. The people who ran out of the water are returning with others, some dive in, others get out quickly, the curious gather faster than shadows, the cries of the swallows multiply. My brother looks at me. It is difficult to talk about such an intimate matter. He speaks a little louder, hints at our father. Jovina remains silent, does not answer, smiles, my brother shouts and suddenly stops, the old woman is deaf. "Oh God, she's not going to understand anything!" The old man has finished with the signatures, gets up from the table, it is he now who is asking questions. My brother and I try to explain, the old man translates our confused words, Jovina Veras confuses our father with someone else with the same name. "Where are Isabe's things? Her pictures?" Who answers? "We're scrupulous people. The deceased has a son in Rio, another in Acre. Death is always followed by disorder. The pictures were scattered on the floor, on the chairs, the neighbors' children even ripped some up.

We gave some away, four or five went to the farm, then we made two packages of the others and sent them to our nephews." "Wasn't there one of a first communion, a group of boys?" "Who knows? It's possible." "Are there any left?" "No." They fished the child's body out of the sea, the shadows of the people who are approaching recoil in fear, the shadows of those who prefer not to see form a circle around him, I get up and look at the find, the sea advances on the beach, a few steps from the dead child I hear the birds crying inside him, hundreds of swallows (trapped, hungry, irate, cruel) wounding each other with their wings, devouring each other with their beaks, screeching inside his body.

⊘ Renato and the others come back, sit down and argue, we start moving again. They are hopeful, someone said he saw a lost boy, the description does not correspond to Renato's child but everybody thinks it is inaccurate and even wrong. I have come back to the surface, I struggle in the mud and manage to lean against the steep bank. My body feels heavy, I barely have the strength to pull myself up, with all the water and dirt I have in my pockets and inside my shirt. We reach the bridge crossing one of the branches of the Capibaribe, here made bigger by the waters of the Pina and the Tejipió. My companions look at the river in silence. Several children have fallen asleep against their fathers' shoulders.

∧ The coral formations come together little by little. I will open the door. Following the line of the equator, but never going beyond the tropics, and always where the water is shallower, the mother-of-pearls spread in the sea. I will open the door, maybe I will see my son. Drawn by this sort of city, which every day becomes more luminous, turbulent and ferocious, many animals migrate to it. I will open the door, maybe I will see my son and laugh off all my fears.

$\oslash$ I have managed to climb the wall—almost losing one of my nails—and throw up kneeling on the ground. My shoes are floating, one is upside down. I try to take off my tie, which is choking me; I get it, throw it in the mud too. I pull out of my pocket a handkerchief half-dry between the folds, wipe my face. I want to wipe my hands but the handkerchief has vanished, I do not know where I put it. My hair is full of dirt, twigs and shreds of vegetation. I look for my comb, but I do not have it any more. My wallet is swollen, I pull it out with difficulty, squeeze the water out against the wall. It looks like a sponge. Z.I. still has not come, nobody else either, no help. I wonder what time it is. I run my hand down my wrist: I lost my watch. Go home, tell some lie, or say nothing at all, wash down to my guts. I look where I think I put my wallet and cannot see it any more. Nobody has passed, not even a dog. A rat maybe? A gust of wind? There is no wind; it must still be where I left it. I feel my pockets for the lighter (with a little light I will certainly find it) and discover that my thirteen pockets are full of mud, and mud only. My money, I.D., lighter, comb, handkerchief, glasses, watch,

a gold chain, the wedding ring, it is all gone, I cannot
even see the album and the shoes floating in the black
water. One night I woke up and lay in bed without
moving, I distinctly heard a rustling of wings against
my shoulder, short dried-up wings. "Is it the Devil who,
deceived, thinking I'm asleep, is hovering in the dark?"
I fell asleep almost immediately, life went on. On the
bank of the canal, stripped of everything as if by some
malicious power, I believe in those wings again and
start to cross myself. I do not have the time to finish:
my wife stands two steps away from me, looking at me.
After having made sure that the ghost in front of her is
me, she turns and walks away without saying a word. I
see myself hugging her, covering her with dirt, sobbing and biting her dress at the height of her shoulder, while she remains silent and stiff, untouched by
my affliction and my pleas. Finally she says: "Don't ever
come back. You'll never see my daughters again. For
us, you'll always be as filthy as you are now." I move
away nauseated by my own misery, my head hanging.
When I raise it, I see the silhouettes of two women
moving away, and one of them is z.i. I holler her name,
follow her wounding my feet, they both begin to run,
I advance resolutely, grab her by her arm. "I love you!"
She turns, spits in my face. Then I see—I saw—I see
then that she is made out of animals pieced together. I
hear a muffled sound, a fluttering of wings, z.i. comes
apart and turns into night birds, wasps, butterflies,
beetles and bats.

∞ We, who have lost so much, form a circle around this boy. We, who have sought so long, found this dead body, a victim of the sea in a city wrested from the sea. Here we were, come from all points of Recife, a fluviomarine plain, surrounded by hills of sand and clay, left by the sea in the Pliocene, when it withdrew from the continent. How many times were the streets we live on and where, in moments of delusion, we imagine we live safely, how many times were they flooded by the sea—once curbed by the hills that nowadays surround the city? Were not those reefs, whose sharp edges rise in the middle of the ocean, litoral cliffs, snatched from the continent by marine assaults? Here we are all around the boy, half-naked, soaked with sun and compassion, breathing the salty air and the light of the early afternoon. We know that we are vulnerable and fragile like him, that our ears are as deaf as his, our eyes as distracted. ▽ My brother visits all the houses on the street where Isabe lived, one by one. Few of the old pictures are left, and none is the one he is looking for. He asks the women, the children, hands out money. Intermingling descriptions arise, all imprecise. Finally, those minds yield to his desire and his frenetic entreaties and someone describes, in great detail, the group of little communicants. This description, which is his own doing, encourages him to continue the search. ⊘ On the bank of the canal, I await the return of the perverse entity that has deprived me of almost everything. It will not be difficult for it to draw close, throw me down to the bottom, this time forever. Perhaps complying with some inflexible code, it demands that the final gesture, that which will consign me to its power without appeal, come from me? I stand with my back turned to the silent waters, looking at the lights of Espinheiro Bridge, shivering with cold, revulsion and misery. Nothing happens. ∧ I will open the door. In hot waters, polyps secrete their hard skeletons. I will open the door, maybe I will see my son. The skeletons form coral reefs and these grow and reach the surface, with their opposing characteristics: refuge and threat. I will open the door, maybe I will see my son, I will laugh off all my fears. Many of the coral reefs form a lagoon, bays, inlets, bristly traps lying in wait for ships; many coral reefs stretch into cordons and fringes, imitating or altering the coastline; many coral reefs take the shape of circular islands, exuberant atolls, oases of green, shade and tranquillity, with their central lake silently responding to the pulsations of the sea. ▽ He goes to the farm of the old man, Isabe's brother. The version according to which some pictures would be there proves to be inaccurate. There is only one: of a French soldier, from the First Great War (Hiquily, Lucien, *brigadier*), with a dedication to Isabe, his unknown patroness from overseas. The rest are color prints, magazine clippings, birthday cards: couples with smooth faces and well contoured lips, with their foreheads touching, in a benevolent world, where petunias blossom in the lovers' hands

and plump birds hover above them with an air of com-
plicity. ∞ Let us weep for the child, we, half men and
half fish, docile amphibians, creatures of uncertainty,
as if we were crying for ourselves. In the course of
time, following the regressions and transgressions of
the sea, the contour of the bay of Recife, changed many
times, altered by the floods of the numerous rivers
(Capibaribe or river of the Capybaras, Tejipió, Jabotão,
Pirapama, Beberibe, Pina, Jiquiá, Camaragibe, Jordão),
coming from far away, or born right here, tributary of
other streams, inscribing and erasing interlaced deltas, many islands, numerous beaches, worlds of sand
banks, kingdoms of crescent-shaped beaches and who
knows how many more deltas. To escape the destiny of
fish, we have been building on the deltas, out of cement, steel, wood, a system of bridges: Maurício de
Nassau, Santa Isabel, Velha, Giratória, Buarque de
Macedo, Boa Vista, Pina, Limoeiro, Derby, Madalena,
Lasserre, Torre, Caxangá—all ten over the canal, and
many others without name or future, collapsed by time,
carried·off by the floods along with trees and animals,
doors and furniture, roofs and dead people, pieces of
us all. Let us weep, then, for ourselves and for the
dead. ⊘ We have almost arrived. The Alfândega quay,
the Santa Rita quay, the old boats, church steeples and
carcasses of trains in the freightyard. Flags blowing in
the wind. In the same boarding-house where I used to
live when I was single, I bathe, get rid of all that filth
that hurts my eyes and even got into my pubic hair.

They lend me a retired colonel's clothes, socks and shoes left behind by an old priest in transit, some money. They ask questions. Without answering, and repeating to myself that if the Devil exists there must be a God too, I wrap my wet clothes in newspaper. I'm going back to the canal. ∧ I will open the door. A colorful world of sponges and actinias lives under the water, among the pillars, arches, beams and porticos of mother-of-pearl; crustaceans nest between the rifts of the caverns, in compact groups; this moveable submarine garden is lit up with red, green, violet and golden reflections; small fish—aquatic butterflies—perform evolutions in cloudlike formations. I will open the door, I will see my son. Starfish patrol that hunting area and eat the fish, the fish eat the flowing manes, the manes eat the crabs, the crabs eat the feathery sea fans, the fans eat the lobsters, the lobsters eat the sunbursts, the sunbursts eat the seahorses, the seahorses eat the boughs, the boughs eat the tip of the stars. I will open the door, I will laugh off all these fears. ▽ He continues to look for the picture, which perhaps got torn or eaten by moths, or lies face down at the bottom of some drawer, among useless papers (in what part of the world?), surrounded by shadows, like our father and the fish that despoiled him of his seaman's garb. ⊘ "If the Devil exists, there must be a God." The package in my arms feels like a dog, like a pig. I walk, in these clothes that are not mine, in these shoes worn by other feet, as if another, a usurper, had appropriated the space

occupied by my body. I throw the dirty clothes into
the channel with anger, thinking that with this gesture
I am getting rid of my weak and hypocritical soul. "Now
I'll wait until another is born within me, blown by the
winds of truth." So many months have passed, and I
am still waiting. And those intimations of truth have
not coalesced. It is difficult to apply an incandescent
iron to our own tumor. ∞ Let us weep hand in hand
around the dead boy—in whom we see ourselves—let
us weep our salty tears. The water always at our side
and always ready to return and submerge all that is
ours, reaches the names of the places we inhabit, few
of which are unfamiliar with this presence. This is the
way the Afflicted neighborhood is, this is the way the
Beberibe or river of the parakeets is, Recife the reef,
the island of Refuge, Milk Island, the Jiquiá or fishing
basket, the island of Good Views, Long Waters, Ibura
or the source, Iputinga or the place of the clear fountain, the Uchoa bridge, the sections of Lowlands, Sands,
Cold Water, the island of Santo Antônio, small river
Parnamirim, and the Little Fishes, the Well, the
Drowned. How many times have we been invaded,
flooded, ravaged by seas whose names we do not know?
How many times have we disappeared and, always stub-
born, rebuilt city, cape, dune, reef, swamp? We have
lost much, losing we live, letting go of what we have,
earn and own, breaking, squandering, putting away,
not finding, using, shattering what is fragile, shredding
the hardiest possessions. For us from Recife, there is

no security, as much as we hold out our arms, trying to preserve the tranquillity of our street. ∧ I get off the bus and many follow me. How many hours pass, between the beginning and the full blooming of a reef? I will open the door, those who are coming with me will wait. Nothing gives away the barrier developing, the structure rising. I will open the door. Will I see my son? Will I laugh off all these fears? While this is happening, the sword is being sharpened, the trap set, the refuge comes into being, the flowers of coral are being born in the sea. One day, along the route followed for so long and where, for many years, it sailed undisturbed, a ship wrecks; one day, preceded by moss, by grass, by ants, by spiders, by grasshoppers, birds, bees, rats, rains and palm trees, a pair of fugitives brings fire, domestic animals, some tools; with them disembark the legions and the invisible choruses that follow or haunt all human beings. My hand reaches out, my eyes are lowered, in the attitude of someone who's going to open that door. I do not hear the slightest sound.

OSMAN LINS

Osman Lins (1924–1978) is one of the most important and innovative writers of contemporary Brazilian fiction. His work has received considerable critical attention both in the United States and abroad and has been translated into several languages. His major works have all been translated into French, German and Spanish; however, only *Avalovara* (1973) has appeared in English to date.

Although Lins began in a more traditional, realistic vein, his later work—*Nine, Novena* (*Nove, Novena,* 1966), *Avalovara* (1973), and *The Queen of the Prisons of Greece (A Rainha dos Cárceres da Grécia,* 1976)—is characterized by formal innovations that reflect the evolution of his poetics and put him on a par with the masters of contemporary Latin American fiction. In addition to his better known fictional works, Lins's production includes several theater pieces and essays.

SUN & MOON CLASSICS

This publication was made possible, in part, through an operational grant from the Andrew W. Mellon Foundation and through contributions from the following individuals and organizations:

Tom Ahern (Foster, Rhode Island)
Charles Altieri (Seattle, Washington)
John Arden (Galway, Ireland)
Paul Auster (Brooklyn, New York)
Jesse Huntley Ausubel (New York, New York)
Luigi Ballerini (Los Angeles, California)
Dennis Barone (West Hartford, Connecticut)
Jonathan Baumbach (Brooklyn, New York)
Roberto Bedoya (Los Angeles, California)
Guy Bennett (Los Angeles, California)
Bill Berkson (Bolinas, California)
Steve Benson (Berkeley, California)
Charles Bernstein and Susan Bee (New York, New York)
Dorothy Bilik (Silver Spring, Maryland)
Alain Bosquet (Paris, France)
In Memoriam: John Cage
In Memoriam: Camilo José Cela
Rosita Copioli (Rimini, Italy)
Bill Corbett (Boston, Massachusetts)
Robert Crosson (Los Angeles, California)
Tina Darragh and P. Inman (Greenbelt, Maryland)
Fielding Dawson (New York, New York)
Christopher Dewdney (Toronto, Canada)
Larry Deyah (New York, New York)
Arkadii Dragomoschenko (St. Petersburg, Russia)
George Economou (Norman, Oklahoma)
Richard Elman (Stony Brook, New York)
Kenward Elmslie (Calais, Vermont)
Elaine Equi and Jerome Sala (New York, New York)
Lawrence Ferlinghetti (San Francisco, California)
Richard Foreman (New York, New York)
Howard N. Fox (Los Angeles, California)
Jerry Fox (Aventura, Florida)
In Memoriam: Rose Fox
Melvyn Freilicher (San Diego, California)
Miro Gavran (Zagreb, Croatia)

Allen Ginsberg (New York, New York)
Peter Glassgold (Brooklyn, New York)
Barbara Guest (Berkeley, California)
Perla and Amiram V. Karney (Bel Air, California)
Václav Havel (Prague, The Czech Republic)
Lyn Hejinian (Berkeley, California)
Fanny Howe (La Jolla, California)
Harold Jaffe (San Diego, California)
Ira S. Jaffe (Albuquerque, New Mexico)
Ruth Prawer Jhabvala (New York, New York)
Pierre Joris (Albany, New York)
Alex Katz (New York, New York)
Pamela and Rowan Klein (Los Angeles, California)
Tom LaFarge (New York, New York)
Mary Jane Lafferty (Los Angeles, California)
Michael Lally (Santa Monica, California)
Norman Lavers (Jonesboro, Arkansas)
Jerome Lawrence (Malibu, California)
Stacey Levine (Seattle, Washington)
Herbert Lust (Greenwich, Connecticut)
Norman MacAffee (New York, New York)
Rosemary Macchiavelli (Washington, DC)
Jackson Mac Low (New York, New York)
In Memoriam: Mary McCarthy
Harry Mulisch (Amsterdam, The Netherlands)
Iris Murdoch (Oxford, England)
Martin Nakell (Los Angeles, California)
In Memoriam: bpNichol
Cees Nooteboom (Amsterdam, The Netherlands)
NORLA (Norwegian Literature Abroad) (Oslo, Norway)
Claes Oldenburg (New York, New York)
Toby Olson (Philadelphia, Pennsylvania)
Maggie O'Sullivan (Hebden Bridge, England)
Rochelle Owens (Norman, Oklahoma)
Bart Parker (Providence, Rhode Island)
Marjorie and Joseph Perloff (Pacific Palisades, California)
Dennis Phillips (Los Angeles, California)
Carl Rakosi (San Francisco, California)
Tom Raworth (Cambridge, England)
David Reed (New York, New York)
Ishmael Reed (Oakland, California)
Tom Roberdeau (Los Angeles, California)

SUN & MOON CLASSICS